THE BREAK

PIETRO GROSSI

THE BREAK

Translated from the Italian by
Howard Curtis

PUSHKIN PRESS

LONDON

Pushkin Press
71–75 Shelton Street
London WC2H 9JQ

Original text © 2007 Sellerio Editore, Palermo
English translation © Howard Curtis 2011

The Break first published in Italian as *L'Acchito* in 2007
This edition first published by Pushkin Press in 2012

5 7 9 8 6 4

This book was translated and published thanks to a generous
translation grant by the Italian Ministry of Foreign Affairs

ISBN 978 1 906548 84 1

Cover Illustration *The Night Café* Vincent Van Gogh
© Yale University Art Gallery 2011

Cover Design © Henry Rivers

Set in 11 on 15 Monotype Baskerville by Tetragon, London
and printed by CPI Group (UK) Ltd, Croydon, CR0 4YY

www.pushkinpress.com

THE BREAK

It is impossible to determine simultaneously the position and momentum of a given object with any degree of precision.
Werner Heisenberg's uncertainty principle 1927

Translator's Note

The form of billiards played in this book is what is known as 'Italian billiards' or 'Italian five-pins'. This game is played with only three balls—a white and a yellow cue ball, one for each of the two players, and a red ball, or object ball. Five miniature skittles, or 'pins' are arranged in a diamond-shaped formation—four white pins surrounding a red one—in the centre of the table. This formation is known as the 'castle'.

The table has no pockets. The objective of the game is to knock down one or more of the pins by getting either one's opponent's ball or the object ball to hit the castle. Points are awarded according to which and how many of the pins are knocked down.

Chapter One

THE BALL SET OFF, as soft as a bread roll, towards the opposite cushion, lightly touched the ball to its right, and before stopping a few inches from the castle sent the opposing ball straight into the red pin, which tipped over onto the baize as if by chance.

"OK, Cirì," Dino said, quickly rubbing his cue with the blue cloth and putting it back in the rack behind him. "I think I'll go home."

"Already?" Cirillo said, setting up the pins again with two fingers and putting the balls back in position.

"Yes, it's not my night tonight."

"Because you're not winning?"

"Don't be stupid, Cirì."

Cirillo gave a half-smile and watched Dino put on his old light-brown leather jacket, which was all threadbare by now. He had never seen him wear anything else. "It's never a good idea to go home earlier than usual," he said.

"I know," Dino said. He turned away, walked to the far end of the room and raised a hand to say goodbye. As he passed, two young guys at the last table but one lowered their heads slightly by way of goodbye, and when Dino put his foot on the bottom step of the stairs they moved closer together and whispered something to each other.

The days were already drawing in. It was the beginning of that time of year when, as evening fell, people seemed to be wandering through a darkened theatre. A man and a woman waved to Dino as they passed, and he replied with as little energy as possible. That was something he'd never been crazy about, greeting people in the street—it was like someone suddenly coming into the bathroom without asking permission, but someone you couldn't reprimand.

During the day, when he was at work, it was different, it was as if, there, his world was everyone's world. There, he liked to stop for a few seconds at the side of the road for a chat, or else if someone passed and happened to wave to him he would calmly get to his feet and raise his arm and return the greeting, with a smile on his face, just as you were supposed to. If those same people met him later on, though, on his way home from the billiard parlour for instance, without his work clothes, they would wonder if something had happened to him, or if he was just plain rude and stand-offish. But that was something else entirely, and even Dino couldn't quite explain it.

When Dino got home, Sofia was at the far end of the living room, making soup at the kitchenette, surrounded by steam and sliced vegetables.

"Hi," Dino said.

Sofia turned with soiled hands, a look of surprise on her face. "Oh," she said. "You're early."

"Yes, it wasn't my night," Dino said.

"Weren't you winning?" Sofia asked, turning away again, and although she had her back to Dino, he knew there was an ironic smile hovering on her lips.

"No," Dino said, "I wasn't winning." He hung his thread-bare old jacket on one of those ugly pieces of pine that a few years earlier he had convinced himself would look good stuck on the wall as a coat rack.

"It isn't a good idea to come home earlier than usual," Sofia said.

"Has Cirillo been here?" Dino asked, almost irritably.

"No, why?" Sofia said, turning for a moment.

"No reason," Dino said, and he went to the wooden table in front of the little kitchenette and sat down on the chair furthest from the door. For a while they were both silent, Dino playing with the grain of the table and Sofia finishing the soup. For some reason, it had always made him feel good, being close to each other like this but slightly distant, and not talking. By the time Sofia brought over the dishes, Dino had already started making a little furrow in the wood.

"Stop that," Sofia said as she put the pot down on the table, on the thin piece of cork Dino had bought a few months earlier. "It's minestrone."

That wasn't a bad idea, Dino thought, but for some reason he didn't feel like saying it out loud.

They ate in silence, both sucking the soup from their spoons as softly as they could and playing their old game of trying to see shapes in the vegetables.

After dinner, Dino and Sofia took the plates to the kitchenette, then Sofia came back carrying an apple and a knife with a wooden handle, and put them down in front of Dino.

Dino looked at her with raised eyebrows.

"I got them from Doni," Sofia said. "They're good."

He looked at the apple, slightly glumly, then made up his mind, gave a slight nod and started peeling it.

"Listen," Sofia said, after a few moments' silence in which the only noise was the sound of his knife cutting through the peel. "I'm pregnant."

Dino had cut off a piece of apple with his knife, and now, holding it with his thumb on the blade, he stopped just as it was going in his mouth. Then, having bitten and chewed the piece of apple for a few seconds, he said, "Oh."

Sofia also started to peel an apple, making a continuous strip that curled round, the way Dino liked it.

Dino tried to keep chewing his apple, but suddenly it was as if one of those hot winds from the south, one of those winds full

16

of sand, was blowing through his teeth and making his mouth dry. "But didn't they say it wasn't possible?" he said, pouring himself a glass of water, his hand a bit less steady than usual.

"They must have been wrong," Sofia said.

Dino looked at his wife for a moment, then lifted the glass and took two or three long gulps. Then he put the glass down again on the table and sat looking at it for a few seconds. "Well?" he asked eventually.

"Well what?"

"Well, what are we going to do?"

Sofia looked at him in silence. She seemed slightly puzzled. "I think we're going to have a baby," she said.

Dino thought about it for a second. "Oh," he said again.

They sat in silence for a while, concentrating on their apples, with their thoughts dancing a jig in front of their eyes.

"What about the travelling we were going to do?" Dino asked, realising suddenly that years had passed, and then more years, and he had long left his youth behind him, and yet had never travelled, not even when he was young and free and not a father.

"Dino," Sofia said. "We've never been anywhere, where do you think we're going to go now?"

Dino nodded slowly, then, with his head still half in the clouds, put the knife and what was left of the apple down on the table, planted a kiss on his wife's forehead, and went and put his jacket back on.

Chapter Two

B Y THE TIME Dino walked back into the room full of
green tables, all of them lit, the young guys who had
waved to him earlier had already gone. Pairs of men had
taken the last tables at the far end of the room, and one pair
were talking just slightly louder than they should.

Cirillo saw Dino walking slowly between the tables, with
his hands in the pockets of his jacket as usual, and immediately realised that something had happened. "I told you
you shouldn't have gone home earlier than usual," he said.

Dino gave a slight smile, along with a little laugh that came
from somewhere inside his chest. "I'll take seven," Dino said,
going to the display case and taking out his cue.

"No game?" Cirillo asked, seeing Dino walk away.

"Not tonight, Cirì, thanks all the same," he heard Dino
say, already with his back to him.

Dino got to Table Seven, turned on the light switch under
the scoreboard, took the little tray with the pins and the

three balls from the drawer and put it down on a corner of the table. Then he picked up the blue cloth, sat down at the edge of the table and started calmly polishing the balls. It was something he almost never did, even though he liked doing it. He liked wiping away those little blue chalk marks from other people's games, games he would never know the end of anyway. It was as if those balls were being wiped clean of the world and becoming new again.

Dino dropped the shiny clean ball on the green baize, got up from the table, grabbed the little tray and turned it over, spilling the pins into his hand, then put the tray back in its place. Usually when he shot a few balls for himself he only put down the central red pin, so that he didn't have to stand the pins back up again every time, but that evening he wanted everything to be just right.

Once he had put all five pins of the castle in their places, he picked up the blue cloth again, wiped the whole of the cue with it, then took an almost new piece of chalk and stroked the tip of the cue with it a couple of times, looking down at the green surface of the table and the three balls, that spider's web of perfect geometries in which bad luck and the evil gods had no place. That was the way it was, at the billiard table—bad luck didn't exist. If you got a shot wrong, if the balls didn't come out the way you wanted or your own ball ended up in the castle, it was because you'd made a bad shot, not because of the gods or bad luck. On the other hand, it sometimes happened that even if you hadn't made the shot the way you should have, your ball went the right way, and even, if fate was really smiling on you, ended up in the cover on the other side of the pins, out of reach of the opposing ball. When that happened, it was called stealing, but no one had ever suggested that it didn't count. When you came down to it, it was comforting to know that there was a place covered in green baize, one hundred and forty-two centimetres wide by two hundred and eighty-four centimetres long, not much more than four square metres, where bad luck had no place, where if you were good you managed to keep the gods under control and, if things worked out well, even let them give you a little nudge.

But that wasn't why Dino was here every night—it had been a long time now that he had been getting the balls to go where he wanted, without needing to control any gods or curse his good or bad luck. Dino was here because he needed things to be clear and precise, to know where they were going to end, to know that there was still a piece of the world where lines and forces and movements followed exact trajectories, without frills, without flights of fancy.

Dino put the piece of chalk to one side, grabbed the cue from the bottom end and touched the lighter-coloured ball with the tip, moving it ever so slightly in his direction. There was something electric in that *clack* produced by the contact

21

of the cue and the ball, a vibration that, for a second, shook the world and made you feel more human. He remembered when as a child, without his aunt knowing, he would go with his dad from time to time to play a couple of games. He hadn't been particularly fascinated—as a friend of his had confessed years later he had been—by the sight of all those men joking among themselves, surrounded by a fog of cigarette smoke and the litter of wine bottles. He had found nothing to admire in those red noses and those yellowed teeth and those swollen bellies. What Dino hadn't been able to take his eyes off was the surface of the table—those hands forming a bridge on the baize to support the cue, those perfectly polished pieces of wood moving like silk over those hard, calloused workers' hands, that clacking of the cues on the surface of the balls and that sharp but muted noise of the balls hitting each other and rebounding off the cushions, that imperceptible sound of the pins as they were knocked down by the balls and fell on the baize. And above all, the automatic, elegant movements of the men at the table. It was as if there, on that green fragment of the world, each man found his own dignity.

Dino stretched across the baize, placed his hand very close to one of the balls, laid the cue across it and moved it backwards and forwards a couple of times, then let it slide until it touched the ball, which slowly rolled across the table, rebounded off the furthest cushion and returned to its starting position, neither a millimetre more nor a millimetre less, no further to the right, no further to the left, but the exact same point from which it had started.

That was the first thing Cirillo had told him to learn. Dino had got it into his head that there was nobody else from whom he'd rather learn the secrets of billiards. To Dino, Cirillo was the only one who mattered, he was the master—a skinny little man with long hair like a gypsy, who beat everyone and held the cue as if it were made of crystal and stroked the balls as if they were a baby's cheeks. Dino was there every minute of his free time, making shots that were askew at best with kids his own age who shot them even more askew than he did, and every minute that he spent there he would glance over at Cirillo and watch how he moved, how he held the cue, how he used the chalk, how he looked at the table before leaning across it to shoot. He would try to understand what secret, what magical mysterious alchemy there was in stroking the balls that way. Until, one day, he had come to the conclusion that he had to have him as his teacher, that the world had no meaning without his guidance, that the answer to all questions—what questions they were he didn't even know himself—were inescapably to be found in the perfect geometries created by that thin, long-haired man. He had spent three months trying to speak to him—he was ashamed to go over to his table, especially with his friends all around him, so every evening he waited, following his every move, hoping to find a moment, a split second, when Cirillo walked off by himself or was alone at his table. But it never came, and every evening, when Dino had to return home to avoid a thrashing from his aunt or his father, Cirillo would still be there, calmly playing with his friends.

Dino would go home every evening feeling dispirited, with his hands in the pockets of the jacket even then—a habit that would stay with him all his life—kicking whatever ball or newspaper he found in the street. Until, one evening, already with one foot on the bottom step of the stairs and his hands in the pockets of his jacket and a dispirited expression on his face, he had told himself that he would never get an opportunity to ask Cirillo to be his teacher, and that if he didn't learn to take things into his own hands he would die waiting. He had turned, crossed the room and walked up to Cirillo's table. A couple of boys Dino's age were still there, finishing a game and smoking to feel more adult, and when they saw Dino walking resolutely towards Cirillo's table, they had turned to each other with puzzled looks on their faces and ironic half-smiles and wondered what the hell he was doing.

"Will you teach me to play?" Dino had blurted out when he was close to the table.

The man who was playing against Cirillo, standing on the other side of the table with the cue in front of him, and all the others sitting around holding glasses of wine, had started laughing in unison, as if Dino had come out with the wittiest remark in the world. Cirillo, who was already leaning across the table, ready to shoot, had turned his head ever so slightly to look at this boy with his combed hair and his funny jacket, who had dared disturb him as he was playing. For a brief but intense moment, Dino had seriously wondered what the hell had come over him. Nobody his age had ever dared go anywhere near that table at the far end of the room, protected as it was behind walls of myth and legend, and populated by men with names you might find in books: Ninetto, Darkie, Gianni Hashish, the Barber. It was an inaccessible place, a country that didn't exist and that certainly shouldn't be disturbed for any reason—it was Mount Olympus, and even just knocking at the door of that realm of the gods was a step too far. And now not only had Dino gone there of his own accord, crossing that imaginary border beyond which nobody his age was ever supposed to venture, but he had disturbed Cirillo in person, the undisputed monarch of that kingdom. And he had disturbed him at the very moment he was about to shoot. And anyone who knows anything at all about billiard parlours, whether they're filled with legendary figures who live in fortresses or not, knows that there are not many rules that have to be obeyed, that it's a place where, all in all, a human being can think of himself as relatively free, but that there is one rule everybody respects—do not disturb. Keep still, talk quietly, because people are there to play billiards and basically that's a serious thing.

Cirillo had looked at Dino for another second, then had turned back to his ball and had started again moving the cue back and forth.

"Go home, son," he had said. "It's late."

Dino had stood there looking at Cirillo, who was sliding that cue with an arm that seemed to have a separate existence, and from somewhere deep inside his head he had heard a voice screaming at him to leave.

"Please," he had said.

This time, nobody had laughed, and everyone had looked, first at that insolent boy who wasn't funny any more, then at Cirillo, who had lowered his head a few centimetres and turned it slightly to one side, then had moved his eyes back to the boy.

"I'm shooting," Cirillo had said, with almost skittish annoyance.

"I know," Dino had said. "I'm sorry. But I absolutely want you to teach me how to play billiards."

"I don't give lessons," Cirillo had said, still bent over the cue, and for a moment he had felt a bit stupid, and didn't know if it was because of the position he was speaking from or because he couldn't somehow bring himself to kick the boy out. Sometimes, when you're a king, you forget what it's like to be out on the streets, you get used to the words and daily rituals of the court surrounding you, so that when a boy gets through the walls and approaches you with the most banal of questions, you don't know what to do and what to say. But if you aren't stupid, a part of you admires that boy, even if it's only because he managed to get to you.

"I know," Dino had said. "I don't want lessons. I want you to teach me how to play."

For a moment, Cirillo had wondered if it was right for the boy to be so familiar with him, but he had preferred not to think about it. He had stood up from the table, had turned to the boy in the funny jacket and looked him up and down for a few seconds.

"Let's do something," Cirillo had said, with a self-satisfied little-smile, like a monarch who, passing a beggar, throws him some of his food, while those around him applaud proudly. "Come back when you can make a break shot, aiming straight ahead of you, and manage to get the ball to come back to exactly the same spot it started from, neither a millimetre more nor a millimetre less, no further to the right, no further to the left."

The boy had looked Cirillo straight in the eyes. "All right," he had said. "Thank you."

"Don't mention it," Cirillo had whispered, still with that half-smile of ironic annoyance. Then he had leant across the table again and shot a ball that hit three sides of the table, his opponent's ball and the red ball, which in turn hit the pins and ended in the cover, scoring four points.

Dino had stopped playing with his friends. Every day they would see him by himself at a table, shooting one break shot after another, just that, never anything else. Sometimes he would curse, and every evening, when he put the cue back in one of the racks and set off for home with his hands in his pockets, he would shake his head disconsolately. Until, one evening, half-an-hour after he had arrived, one of his friends saw him there with his hands propped on the side of the table staring at the ball with a self-satisfied smile. Dino had put the cue down, turned and very calmly crossed the whole room, as if all at once it was half his, all the way to Cirillo's enchanted castle, just as Cirillo was leaning across the table, ready to shoot.

"I did it," Dino had said, very pleased with himself, as soon as he came level.

This time, Cirillo was on the other side of the table, and in order to see where that voice had come from he simply had to raise his head a little. He had stopped moving his cue and stared at Dino.

"Shit, son," he had said. "Do you always have to bother me when I'm shooting?"

"I'm sorry," Dino had said. "But I did it."

Cirillo had thrown him another brief, slightly annoyed glance, then looked down again at his cue, moved it back and forth two or three times then slid it forward gently until it kissed the ball, which first hit the cushion with a muffled sound that was little more than a breath, then knocked the opponent's ball straight through the middle of the castle, toppling only the red one.

"Every time?" Cirillo had asked, even before straightening up after the shot, with the confident bearing of someone who is about to land the decisive blow.

Dino had looked Cirillo straight in the eyes for a few seconds. All the confidence that had transported him like a leaf across the room had suddenly abandoned him, and for some reason his legs had seemed harder and heavier than usual.

"No," Dino had said. "Only once."

A hollow-cheeked man sitting not far from them with an unfiltered cigarette in his hand had started to laugh, smoke blowing out between his teeth, but Cirillo had glared at him and made him stop.

"Come back when you can do it every time," Cirillo had said.

Dino and Cirillo had looked at each other for a moment longer, as stiff as marble statues, across the only battlefield they knew.

"All right," Dino had said in a thin voice, then he had lowered his head and left the field with head bowed.

Cirillo had watched him walk to the far end of the room and disappear up the stairs with his hands stuck as always in his pockets.

"It's my turn, can I?" Cirillo had heard a voice say to his right. On the other side of the table, Torello, who wore glasses and always looked as if he was retarded, was waving his cue.

"Yes, go on," Cirillo had said, and with a little sigh had put his hand down on the table and resumed the game.

Chapter Three

DINO HEAVED A DEEP SIGH, then touched the ball with the tip of his cue and moved it slightly to the left. The other ball was beyond the castle, towards the top left-hand corner. Dino moved for just a moment to the right, then to the middle, sizing up the distances, using the castle as a point of reference. He stroked the tip of the cue with the chalk, leant over with his bridge hand in front of the ball and the cue lying on top of it, moved the cue backwards and forwards, making sure to get the ball well to the left in order to give it the proper spin and finally released his elbow and the two fingers of his right hand that were holding the cue. The ball set off, rolling straight ahead as if it had never stopped or started anywhere but had always been moving. It hit the first cushion, *thump*, then the second, *thump*, and, because of the spin he had given it, rebounded directly into the other ball. *Clack.* The other ball immediately set off as if in a relay race and rolled straight and smooth towards the castle, hitting the central red pin and the white pin on the other side and stopping about ten centimetres beyond the castle. There is something majestic about a shot that goes exactly the way it is supposed to, something that breaks through the squalor of the world and for a moment makes you feel more refined.

Holding the cue in his left hand, Dino leant across the table and set the fallen pins back up again, then he walked around to where the chalk was, picked it up and stroked the tip of the cue with it a few times, looking in silence at the balls and the table.

A short distance away, three boys laughed among themselves as they put on their coats and drained the last drop of wine from their glasses.

Dino again walked around the table, looking closely at the balls, and stopped next to the long side, the side where his own ball was. He lowered himself, placed the cue across his bridge hand, which was relatively close, and moved his body backwards and forwards a bit. As they were walking towards the far end of the room, the three boys in coats, still with amused half-smiles on their lips, stopped for a moment not far from Dino's table. One of the three moved his head closer to the other two and whispered something, indicating Dino with his chin.

The ball moved away from the cue as if of its own accord, rolled as far as the long cushion opposite, rebounded off it as if pushed by a sudden gust of wind, and hit the short side and then the other cue ball, which set off towards the third cushion, rebounded and moved very calmly, almost whistling, towards the castle. It passed straight through the middle, knocking out the central red pin and one white pin on the other side, and then immediately came to a stop.

The three boys looked at each other for a moment, then went out, sniggering and again whispering something.

Very slowly, Cirillo started to close up, cleaning and tidying the tables until everyone had gone and the only patch of light in the room came from his friend's table. He had been watching Dino all evening, as he played one shot after another and knocked down the pins with the pensive calm of an angler fishing from a lake.

In all the time he had been closing up, Cirillo had done his best not to disturb his friend, even doing a few things he had been putting off for several days to spin out the time. Now he walked slowly to Dino's table and leant against one of the pillars that supported the room.

Dino released the cue. The ball set off quite quickly, hit three cushions and then the other cue ball, sending it straight into the pins and stopping a few centimetres beyond the castle.

Cirillo had often watched Dino playing alone. A year earlier, he had even stood there watching him for an entire evening, without Dino noticing. And every time he

33

watched him play, he wondered if Dino would ever beat him. It was hard to say, but one thing was certain—if it did ever happen, it would be a great game. Thinking about it, Cirillo couldn't really figure out why it was that Dino had never managed to beat him—he never missed a shot, always got in the cover. If you looked closely—not that he would ever admit it—Cirillo actually made a few more mistakes than Dino did. And yet, when they came to add up the points, Cirillo's shots always scored more, and by the end of the game they weighed in the balance like blocks of granite.

Dino hit another ball that rebounded off three cushions and sent the other cue ball straight into the castle.

"Tell me one thing, Cirì," Dino said when he had straightened up, although without taking his eyes off the table. He walked to the other side, lowered himself in front of the other ball and sent it rebounding off two cushions and knocking the other cue ball back into the castle. "How many stones do you think it takes to make a person?"

Cirillo screwed up his eyes for a moment, then gave his friend a puzzled look. "What do you mean?" he said.

Dino again stretched across the table and moved the cue backwards and forwards for a moment or two. "To make a person, a human being, how many stones would you say it takes?"

The ball moved away from the cue with a little murmur. *Thump*, first cushion. *Thump*, second cushion. *Clack*, ball. *Flop*, pins. In the silence and emptiness of the room, it sounded like music.

Dino and Cirillo had looked at each other for a few seconds.

"I don't know, son," Cirillo had said. "But the road is long."

Chapter Four

DINO STOPPED FOR A MOMENT in front of the crumbling facade of an old building, looked around him on the ground and picked up some pieces of a broken bottle. Then he looked up and threw a piece of glass at one of the blue shutters at the front of the building. The small piece of glass hit the wall next to the shutter and broke into pieces.

"Rosa!" Dino whispered as loudly as he could, then fell silent and waited with the pieces of glass in his hand. A man passed him, dressed to the nines, and his footsteps echoed on the pavement like the ticking of a clock.

Dino watched the man move along the street and disappear round the corner, then looked again at the shutter towards which he had thrown the piece of glass. He stood looking at it for a few seconds, then selected a slightly bigger piece, and after looking around—with the hint of a smile on his lips which took him back years—again threw it towards the building, harder this time, and this time the glass hit the slats of the shutter, making a bit of a noise.

Dino gave a slight boyish laugh, dipped his head between his shoulders for a moment, then looked around again. Nobody was passing. There was a thin sliver of moon in the sky, occasionally obscured by clouds.

"Rosa!" he whispered again as loudly as he could.

After a few seconds, a sharp noise of creaking iron filled the silence of the street, and the shutters opened, but only a crack.

"Who is it?" came a quiet voice from behind the shutters.

"Rosa," Dino said, "I need a rose."

"Piss off, you hooligans," the voice said, and the shutters knocked loudly against each other, followed again by that sharp sound of creaking iron, more forceful this time.

"No, Rosa, wait, it's Dino."

"Dino who?" the voice behind the closed shutters said.

"Dino Dino."

"The stone-layer?"

"Yes, the stone-layer."

For a few seconds, silence filled the street again, to be broken once more by that sharp noise of creaking iron, and at last the shutters opened and the pale, lined face of an old woman appeared. The woman was barely tall enough to be seen above the windowsill, and her face, surrounded by a halo of unkempt white hair, was framed in the window like a picture that has been badly hung.

"Aren't you ashamed, still playing these stupid jokes at your age?" Rosa said in a low voice.

When they were boys, after an evening spent in some bar or other, dreaming of women's breasts and knocking back cheap wine, they would invariably stop in front of Rosa's window on their way home, throw a few stones or pieces of broken glass or anything else they could find, and when she asked who it was they would all cry, as if it was a password, "Rosa, give us a rose!" and laugh like idiots. Sometimes they even sang a little chorus. It was like a perfect end to a drunken evening, that last idiotic joke which sent them to bed happy, and for some reason, if they didn't do it, then the day after they would wake up even more hung-over.

Every time, Rosa would cry "Piss off, you hooligans!" and slam the shutters shut. But the next time, she would still ask who it was.

Oddly, Rosa had been old even then.

"No, Rosa, I really do need a rose."

"Go home, Dino. And stop drinking, you're too old for that."

"Rosa, I'm as sober as a judge."

"Goodnight, Dino."

"Rosa, wait, Sofia's expecting a baby."

Rosa had already reached out an arm as thin as a stick towards the shutter. "Really?" she said, looking Dino right in the eyes.

"Really. She told me this evening."

Rosa let go of the shutter and put her arm back behind the windowsill. "Poor woman," she said.

"What do you mean, 'poor woman'?" Dino said, his smile a little strained for a moment.

"Well," Rosa said, "with a husband like you … "

"Go to hell, Rosa," Dino said.

Rosa's head gave a little jump in the darkness of the window, and a stifled, barely perceptible giggle briefly filled the silence of the street.

"Anyway," Rosa said, "what are you doing walking the streets at this hour and in that condition if your wife is pregnant?"

"I'm not drunk."

"Of course you're not," Rosa said. "Not that it makes any difference."

"I don't know," Dino said, playing with one of the pieces of glass he was still holding. "It's just that she told me about the baby and I wasn't expecting it … They told us we … Then we made other plans … I don't know, Rosa, I went out to play billiards. And that's why I'm taking her a rose."

Dino and Rosa looked each other in the eyes for a few seconds.

"What an idiot," Rosa said. "Wait there and don't move."

For a moment Rosa's thin little arm reappeared, and a moment later the shutters knocked together, followed immediately by the usual noise of creaking iron.

Dino stood there, stiffly, a moment or two longer, staring at the wall of the building, then he turned and, still playing with the pieces of glass he had in his hand, went and sat down on the pavement on the other side of the street. It was strange that there was nobody passing tonight—usually groups of youths, or the odd nightbird, gave a dash of colour to the streets, but tonight a pall of inertia seemed to have fallen over everything. Maybe people had lost the habit.

After a while, the rolling shutter of Rosa's shop started to open, and beneath it two thin little legs appeared, then what looked like an old reddish dressing gown. The shutter rose just over a metre until Rosa's head appeared. She peered out and looked straight at Dino.

"Come on, then, delinquent," Rosa said, motioning to him with a curt gesture of the arm and disappearing again into the darkness behind the shutter.

Dino leapt to his feet and walked quickly across the road, looking around as if he was about to commit a robbery and someone had opened a back door for him.

"You shouldn't open the shutter by yourself," Dino said when he was inside.

"And you shouldn't be wandering the streets drunk at this hour," Rosa said, lifting the oil lamp she had in her hand

41

to get a better look at Dino. She looked him up and down and shook her head without saying a word, then turned with the lamp towards the masses of plants and flowers that filled the shop.

"Let's see," Rosa said, "what you need is—"

"I was thinking—"

"You shut up," Rosa said. "You don't know anything about these things."

Rosa's lamp roamed the shop. The place was a riot of leaves and colours and scents which quickly went to the head.

"Ah, here we are," Rosa said suddenly, in that old lady voice of hers. She stooped over a row of little green bushes, holding the lamp behind her to keep her balance. For a moment Dino was afraid she would fall on the floor or break in two as she stooped.

Sighing with the effort, Rosa plunged her hand into a vase of tall, multicoloured roses. When, with a deep sigh of relaxation, she pulled her hand out again, it was clutching the long, sturdy stem of a huge red rose. Dino couldn't remember ever seeing anything like it—the stem was more like a tree trunk, and the flower, which had lots and lots of big shiny petals, would be hard to hold even with both hands.

"Where did you find that?"

Rosa threw a glance at Dino, with a hint of a smile, then gazed at the flower. "There are things it's better not to know," she said as if it was some illegal substance.

Rosa went behind the wooden counter, put the huge flower down on top of it, picked up a huge pair of shears and in one swift movement cut a few inches from the stem.

Dino gave a start and screwed up his eyes.

"Don't worry, it's good for it," Rosa said, putting the shears aside.

Then she took two or three branches of greenery from a vase next to it, dressed it with something that looked like lily of the valley, wrapped everything in a sheet of coarse paper, and put a red satin ribbon around it.

"Go," Rosa said, turning the stem of the flower towards Dino. "You'll be fine with this. It's better than a bunch of twenty-five normal roses."

Dino took the flower in his hand and thanked Rosa. For a moment, he felt quite moved. "What do I owe you?" he asked.

"Go home, it's late," Rosa said, pushing him towards the exit. "And kiss that poor woman for me."

As Dino was about to leave, bending to get under the shutter, he took a last look at the old lady in her dressing gown. "Rosa," he said, "don't you wear dentures?"

"I'll give you dentures, idiot," Rosa said, and to force him out landed a kick with her thin little leg in his shin, then slammed the shutter down in his face as hard as she could.

When Dino got home, the silence between the walls seemed thicker than usual. He decided to get undressed in the entrance, and then very slowly eased himself into the bed, trying to make as little noise as possible.

As usual, Sofia was lying on her side, facing the edge of the bed, with her legs slightly bent. Dino slipped in on his side, slid over until he was touching Sofia's back, put his arm round her and laid the big rose right under her nose. The scent of the rose echoed in Sofia's ears like the ringing of twenty bells.

"Hi," Sofia said after a few seconds, moving slightly closer to Dino.

"Hi," Dino whispered in her ear, and added, "I'm sorry," hoping it was the right thing to say.

"Don't worry," Sofia said, her voice still slurry with sleep.

For a few moments silence fell again over the room, and the only thing that could be heard was the rose's scent like a peal of bells.

"You know, don't you?" Dino said after a while, just before they fell asleep.

"Yes, I know," Sofia said, and without letting go of the rose pulled Dino even closer to her.

Chapter Five

D INO COULDN'T GET that damned question out of
his head.

That morning he had got to work as punctually as ever.
Saeed and the others had seen him coming along the street
with his hands in his pockets and his head down. He had
arrived at his usual calm pace, and after greeting them with
a brief nod had started putting his overalls on. They were
resurfacing a wide street that led to the centre of town. They
had already put down a base of earth and fine chippings,
and now they had to water it, lay the stones, and smooth
everything out with the jackhammer.

Dino didn't usually talk while he was working, although
he always seemed fairly cheerful. Often he would whistle,
or hum under his breath, some song he had learnt from
a relative when he was little. It was apparently a habit he
had got half from his aunt, half from his dad—she was
always singing at the top of her voice, while he always

maintained a solid wall of silence that seemed to conceal things bigger than himself. If he thought about it, Dino found both things equally annoying, and obviously, whether he liked it or not, he had taken a little from one and a little from the other.

Today, though, Dino was more like his father. When he had finished putting on his overalls and lacing up his boots, he had sat for a moment with his elbows on his knees, heaved a little sigh and told Duilio and Blondie to smooth out the base one last time and then wash it down with water from the tanker. In the meantime, he and Saeed would start bringing the stones. They had been working together for years and there wasn't really any need to say anything else for the rest of the day.

Blondie had been the last to join them. Nobody had ever discovered where Dino had found him. One day, Dino had simply gone to Giani, the boss, and asked him if he could hire the boy to help out. Giani had looked through the glass door at the thin, blond young man sitting wearily on a wooden bench just outside.

"Why do you need anyone else?" Giani had asked, tidying a few papers on his desk.

"To teach him the trade," Dino had said.

Giani had looked him in the eyes for a moment, then carried on sorting through the papers. "Aren't Duilio and the black guy enough?"

46

"Duilio's getting old, and I don't know how much longer he can last. If he quits, I need someone who already knows the work. Remember the problems we had that time with Giorgione."

Giorgione had died suddenly one night in the middle of February. He had gone to bed at night as if everything was normal and in the morning his wife had found him lying dead beside her. A weak heart, the doctor had told Dino one day when they had happened to find themselves together in a bar. For the first time, it had struck Dino that inside everyone's chest there was an animal with a soul and a personality all of its own, capable or not of withstanding the stresses and strains of the world, and, as he shook the doctor's hand and watched him walk away, he had wondered what kind of animal his was.

Anyway, overnight Dino had found himself working only with Duilio, who to be honest wasn't quite his old self any more. He thought for a whole day about who he could get to replace Giorgone, then he remembered that black bricklayer he had seen once unloading huge weights all by himself and throwing mortar with the trowel at a hole fifteen metres away, hitting it, and laughing with his workmates. The last time he had seen him, though, he had been wasting time drinking in an old-fashioned bar on the other side of town. Dino had gone there and asked the owner about him, and had been pointed to the far end of the room. Saeed was sitting with a half-empty glass in his hand, staring into space. Apparently nobody wanted to give him work, because he was black—or rather, not so much because he was black, but because he wasn't local, and nobody wanted to take work away from local people and give it to foreigners.

"I don't give a damn where you're from. As long as you clean yourself up, stop drinking, and work the way I saw you work on that house on the other side of the river, then you have a job."

Giani wasn't at all sure that Duilio was too old. He had looked out again at the young man sitting on the bench. "Doesn't look too bright to me," he had said, looking again at Dino.

"He's a quick learner, you'll see," Dino had said.

Giani had turned to look at the young man again for a few moments, then looked back at Dino, trying to figure out if there was some kind of ulterior motive.

"Half pay, Dino. That's the best I can do."

"All right," Dino had said, and had shaken Giani's hand and left with the young man.

Nobody, not Duilio, not Saeed, had really looked into whether there was an ulterior motive to the boy's hiring, and, knowing Dino, they knew that asking questions would be a waste of time. In any case, they had soon got used to Blondie's impassivity and his silences and, especially, his great appetite for work.

Dino spent the whole morning bent over the road. On his knees, he wore those big protective pads that Sofia, much to everyone's delight, had sewn for the men. He would bend over the ground, grab a stone, push it into the still partly wet base layer, pick up the small rock hammer, which was quite old and worn now, give the stone a few knocks with it to adjust its position, lay a piece of wood over it to make sure it was level with the others, and if, as was usually the case, it was already fine, he would put down the hammer and grab another stone. And so it went on, stone by stone.

There was no precise logic to the way you placed the stones. It was something that had puzzled him when, still a child, trying to place a stone, he had asked his father what distance from the others it should go.

"Trust your eye," his father had said, in that voice of his that always seemed to be breaking through a wall from another world.

Dino had straightened up and looked at his father with an almost scared expression. "What do you mean, trust your eye?"

He had raised his head and squinted at his son. "That's right, your eye," he had said.

In some strange way that he didn't understand, Dino had realised that something was happening at that moment which would mark him for the rest of his life.

"Isn't there a specific order?" he had asked.

Dino's father had found it strange to hear those words used by a child, especially his own son, and for a moment he had sensed something new and unknown. "No, Dino, there's no specific order," he had said, in a voice that wouldn't have been expected of him.

"Oh," Dino had said, and had watched his father get back to work.

All at once life had taken a different turn. What, up until that moment, he had recognised, consciously or unconsciously, as the world, had turned all at once into a place in which people walked down streets where there was no specific order. From one moment to the next, what Dino had innocently thought of as perfect was flawed by a logic that didn't exist, or at least a logic he didn't know. Gradually, after those first feelings of dismay, undeclared but profound, he had learnt to absorb that revelation, and had even found it more bearable after a time, because, whether you liked it or not, whether you accepted it or not, there still had to be some kind of logic to the laying of those damned stones. Why was it that every time Dino's father looked at a piece of roadway that had been laid by someone else, he could point to a particular spot and say, "That stone isn't straight"? And if you went and had a look at the stone that Dino's father had indicated, you saw that in fact it wasn't straight. You didn't know exactly why or how, and yet if you looked at that stretch of road as a whole, however well surfaced it was, you couldn't deny that in the exact spot indicated by Dino's father, there was a crack, a fissure in that system governed by unknown rules. And so, stone by stone, day by day, year by year, Dino had given up trying to understand the rules of that system, but had somehow found his own place within it and had learnt to lay those damn stones the way they were supposed to be laid.

Dino spent all morning kneeling on the road with Saeed and Duilio, without whistling or humming a song. And at lunchtime, still in silence, he had unwrapped his roll from a large piece of brown paper and had sat down to one side to eat it, without saying a word, occasionally taking a sip of water from a clear glass bottle.

After a while, Saeed and Blondie had gone off somewhere for a coffee and a quick tipple, and Dino and Duilio had stayed there to finish their lunch in silence. Duilio was eating with a fork from a little metal pot prepared for him by his wife and every now and again knocking back a gulp of wine from a flask. Some years earlier, when for some reason Dino had started taking an interest in Duilio's health, he had told him that he shouldn't drink all that wine.

"And you shouldn't drink all that water," Duilio had replied, and that was the end of it.

Dino took another bite of his roll, chewing the crust vigorously and screwing up his face slightly as he did so, and drank some water, then swallowed the whole lump. As he tried to remove a hard piece from his molars he looked up at Duilio and said, "How many stones do you think it takes to make a person?"

Duilio looked up at Dino with a puzzled expression. Duilio was a worker of the old school, all twisted and gnarled and wrinkled like a hundred-year-old, but in his way as tough and strong as a mule, with the kind of straightforward relationship to things, and to the earth, that was on its way out. He was from the same generation as Dino's father, and they had worked together for years, which was what kept Dino and Duilio both united and distant.

"How many stones does it take to make what?" Duilio asked, screwing up his face.

"A person, Duilio." Dino raised his voice. "A PERSON."

"Oh," Duilio said, nodding as if it was a perfectly normal question, then looked off to one side, thought about it for a moment and turned back to Dino with a puzzled look. "A person? What do you mean, a person?"

Dino stuck one finger in his mouth, trying to get to that piece of hard bread, but without much success. "I don't know, Duilio, it's just something that came into my head."

"Oh," Duilio said, looking off to the side again. He sat there for a while, quite still, with his fork stuck in the little pot, staring at the road, while Dino took another bite of his roll.

"A lot, anyway," Duilio said after a while, and continued eating his lunch.

Chapter Six

S OFIA WAS WALKING along the pavement with quick, resolute steps, keeping close to the old stone walls. She turned left into a side street, and walked along it until she reached that small enclosed square which somehow always managed to be in the sun. She came to a large dark wooden door and rang the bell.

After a few moments, the door was opened by a somewhat elderly lady in a white coat with two or three pens stuck in her front pocket.

"Hello," the lady said, standing in the entrance, with her hand on the heavy wooden door.

"Hello," Sofia said.

The two women sized each other up for a few seconds without saying anything.

"Can I help you?" the woman asked, tilting her head slightly to one side.

"I'd like to see the doctor," Sofia said.

The woman frowned slightly. "Do you have an appointment?" she asked, thinking she already knew the answer.

"Yes," Sofia said. "I've had an appointment for nine years."

The lady's head gave a little jerk backwards. She stared at Sofia for a second. "Oh," she said. "Please come in."

The lady in the white coat led her into a hall with rugs on the floor and a little wooden table in a corner, facing the entrance. She then opened a door to her left and asked Sofia to sit down and wait.

The room had a terracotta floor and another rug, a large round one. Along all four walls were chairs of different kinds, and in the middle was a large low table covered in newspapers and magazines. Sofia sat down on the small chair in the corner and placed her bag on her knees.

"Who should I say?" the woman asked, almost embarrassed now.

"Sofia, the dressmaker," Sofia said.

There had been a period, some years earlier, when Sofia and Dino had tried for a long time to have children but nothing had happened.

One morning, as Sofia, silent as always, was wrapping clothes for a lady in the brown paper that Gianni brought her—from where, nobody knew—the lady had said, "My cousin might be able to do something for you."

For the first time in her life, Sofia had felt heat move in a wave from her neck up into her face and tingle like grains of rice beneath her cheeks and her forehead. Months later, when she had seen a young girl blush in the street, she had wondered if that was what had happened to her, too, remembering it as a not very pleasant sensation.

"That'll be seven, and this one's five," Sofia had said to the lady, not even looking her in the eyes.

The lady had calmly handed over the money, then walked away across the terracotta floor with a slight shrug of her shoulders, which Sofia didn't quite know how to interpret.

That evening, on her way home, Sofia had passed the greengrocer's stall. The greengrocer was a small plump woman, who for some reason always came to work in a skirt and evening shoes. Sofia had gone up to the stall and stuck a big sewing needle into an orange as big as a melon.

"The next time I can sew on a mouth and ears," Sofia had said and continued on her way.

The greengrocer had stood there like a stone, looking at that huge needle planted in her orange, and the drop of pulp already starting to trickle down one side. The greengrocer wasn't quite sure why, but that evening, when she returned home, she had put the orange with the needle in it over the fireplace, and there it had stayed.

Sofia had forgotten all about that, and when, a few weeks later, the lady had come back to her shop with the usual blouses and skirts to be mended, she hadn't taken much notice of her.

But she and Dino had still not had a child, and for the first and last time Sofia had wondered if it was right to give life a push in a certain direction instead of taking it as it came. She had thought about it for a few days until she was tired of thinking, and then, one day when the lady came to collect a blouse the neck of which had become threadbare, Sofia had told her that she had thought about it, and that she would be pleased to have her cousin's address. The lady had been caught unawares, and for a moment had looked Sofia straight in the eyes. The two women had confronted one another for a moment like two blockhouses, with that small dark wooden counter between them keeping them at a distance like a trench, silently manoeuvring in a battle that had been going on for centuries.

All at once, the lady had taken a pen and a sheet of paper from her bag and written down her cousin's name and address in tiny round handwriting.

"Tell him I sent you," she had said, looking Sofia straight in the eyes again for a moment. Then she had walked out with a pride and dignity that Sofia had never seen in her before.

Sofia had never paid for that visit or the tests that the lady's cousin—a pleasant, tactful man—had carried out, and the lady had never again paid for a single blouse or a single mend, and their relationship had continued like that, as silent as it had always been, but without the question of money coming into it.

Anyway, what had emerged from the tests was that Sofia couldn't have children. That was what the lady's cousin had told Sofia one morning at the beginning of October, when a cold late summer wind was blowing, bringing with it the first dead leaves and the first autumn rain. The lady's cousin had told her the news with a mixture of sadness and embarrassment in his eyes, which Sofia had not understood immediately. But when she had found herself back out in the street, forced against her will to lift the collar of her coat, and surrounded by people hurrying about their own business, she had felt a kind of inert, nauseating emptiness she didn't quite know how to take, an emptiness which, all things considered, she had never thought she would be able to feel.

In all honesty, Sofia had never had what you might call an easy life. But she had come to the conclusion that that it was pointless crying about it, that life was already enough of a pain in the neck in itself and that you just had to accept it for what it was and not think too much about it. Consciously or unconsciously, she had told herself that she wasn't in charge of the game, and that all she could do was throw the dice and hope she ended up in the right place on the board.

That morning, though, had been different, that morning the cold wind that brought the first leaves of autumn with it seemed to have penetrated her bones and chilled her stomach. When she had got back home, Dino had had the momentary impression that he was looking at another woman, someone different who had put on his wife's clothes.

"It's cold," Sofia had said.

Somehow Dino had realised something, something he couldn't entirely grasp, although he knew in which area it lay. He had taken Sofia, put a thick woollen blanket around her, thrown two or three pieces of wood saved over from the previous winter into the fireplace, and sat his wife in front of the fire. He had decided not to go to work that day and he had started making soup as his aunt had taught him when he was a boy.

"We could go to the Far East," Dino had said a few days later, in the middle of the night.

"What?" Sofia had muttered, thinking that Dino was talking in his sleep again.

"I said, we could go to the Far East."

"The Far East?"

"That's right."

"And what would we do there?"

"I don't know, see how it is. I heard some men talking about it the other day. They said there are entire cities on tops of mountains, and men who sit there all the time like statues, just thinking, and even a place where a king built an entire palace out of marble as white as snow when his wife died, and he wanted to make a black one for when he died, but he died too early. Funny, isn't it?"

"Yes, that is funny," Sofia had said, smiling in the dark.

"We could go and see that palace. What's to keep us here?"

"It sounds like a very good idea," Sofia had said, then they had fallen asleep again, and the next morning they had both gone to work as if everything was normal.

It had become a kind of game—every now and again, one of them would come home with an idea for a new destination, and they would start to get excited about it, as if they were really leaving, and would start imagining the places they would visit and how they would get there and who they would meet. They had even bought a big notebook with a thick coloured cover, where they wrote down everything in preparation for when they left. They had called it *The Travel Book*, which wasn't much of a name when you thought about it, and yet every time they mentioned it or took it in their hands there seemed to be something great about it. Occasionally, when they talked and thought about the places they would visit, Sofia would write something on a large sheet of paper or on a table napkin, then later or the next day you would see her there bent over the table in front of the kitchenette, moving her hand over that coloured notebook and writing down everything she and Dino had told each other. Or at least that was what Dino assumed she was doing—he had never opened the book, not that one or any of the others she had filled over the following years. At first he hadn't opened them because he knew perfectly well what was written in them and remembered the journey they wanted to make to America or black Africa. Then one day, while Sofia was out buying a few things for dinner, he had decided to take a look at all the things that he and his wife had thought up and had taken down one of the notebooks, but, after putting it down on the table with a glass of wine next to it, he had changed his mind, because there seemed to be something bigger in those pages than he had anticipated.

In the end, though, Dino and Sofia had never been to any of those places, and Dino had barely thought about it. From time to time, they would spend a few evenings or a few hours at night fantasising about desolate moors and age-old trees and people in silvery clothes, and the fact that they got up the next morning and everything went on the way it always had left them, all things considered, fairly indifferent. Sometimes, before going to work in the morning, Dino would find himself wondering how many stones he would have to lay before he could afford to go to the North Pole to see those strange white bears and those funny birds with short legs and no wings he had heard about one day from Franco. He would even wonder how many stones it would take to pave a road that would go all the way up there, and as he set off calmly for work his head would be filled with infinite, dizzying galaxies of stones and roads that never ended.

Chapter Seven

"HELLO, DINO," Giani said, coming back into his office with a pile of papers in his hand.

"Hello, Giani," Dino said, sitting on the chair in front of the desk, with his hands placed firmly on the armrests. Dino always sat like that on these chairs, as if he was constantly on the verge of leaping to his feet and running away.

"Paper, nothing but paper," Giani said, dropping the pile of papers on the desk with a great thud. "I'm going to end up drowning in paper."

He sat down, quickly passed his hands through his hair, heaved a deep sigh, let his shoulders droop slightly and looked Dino straight in the eyes. There was something about Giani this morning, a mixture of sadness and restlessness. Dino didn't think he had ever seen him like that before.

"So, Dino, how's it going?" Giani asked with a slight smile.

"Fine, thanks," Dino said, also making an effort to smile.

"I hear you're expecting a baby," Giani said, still with that strange hesitant smile on his face.

"Yes," Dino said with a nod, not quite sure what else to say.

"Why didn't you tell us?"

"No reason," Dino said, shrugging his shoulders and almost imperceptibly spreading his hands. "It just slipped my mind."

Giani nodded, looking at Dino for another moment, then dropped his eyes to the desk and turned a paper clip round and round between his fingers. "Listen," he said. "How's the street coming along?" He didn't sound very convincing.

"Fine," Dino said, looking closely at Giani. "We're almost there. We'll be finished either tomorrow evening or the following morning. By the way, a lady told me we have to redo the stretch along the river."

Giani tapped the paper clip on the table a few times, then shot Dino a brief glance. "That's just it. That's what I wanted to talk to you about."

Dino didn't like Giani's tone. He had no idea why, but thinking about that moment later he would remember it as an actual shock, which had frozen his spine and turned his stomach, like the first time you realise, from something your wife says, that she might be leaving you.

"Go on," Dino said, looking Giani straight in the eyes and trying not to be too defensive.

Giani threw another glance at Dino, then again tapped the paper clip on the desk, a bit louder this time. "Listen,

Dino," he said, sighing slightly, "I need to tell you the way things are. They're going to use asphalt."

For a moment, all Dino could hear was his own heart beating in his chest like a train and in his ears a deep, diffuse sound like the skin of a drum being hit hard.

"What you do mean, they're going to use asphalt?" Dino asked after a while, gripping the arms of the chair tighter and continuing to look Giani in the face.

"Just that," Giani said. "I mean, they're going to use asphalt. No more stones, Dino. The council have decided they cost too much and take a lot of maintenance, and they need the money for other things."

"Like what?" Dino asked sharply, as hard as a block of marble.

Giani looked at Dino for a moment, in the grip of conflicting emotions he couldn't quite sort out. "I don't know, Dino," he said, shaking his head and lowering his eyes. "All I know is that there's nothing I can do about it. No more stones, I'm sorry." He quickly glanced up at Dino then looked down again.

"What about us?" Dino asked after a while, with a determination that would not normally have been expected from him.

Giani straightened the end of the paper clip and let his eyes come to rest on Dino. "Well, Dino, I don't know what to say. The thing is, you're all experts at surfacing streets, not at laying stones. As far as the council are concerned, once you've learnt how it's done, you can keep your jobs, laying asphalt."

Dino was silent for a few seconds, trying to find a way to say what he was thinking without making poor Giani feel guilty, because, when you came down to it, this probably wasn't anything to do with him.

"Fuck off," he said, then stood up and left the room, slamming the door behind him.

"Dino!" Giani shouted from inside his office, while Dino was walking through the outer room with all the secretaries looking at him.

"Shit," Giani said to himself, jerking his head back and throwing the half-twisted paper clip on the desk.

Chapter Eight

THE EVENING CIRILLO had asked him if he succeeded every time, Dino had wondered, as he was on his way home, if life really had to be this way. For the past two months, he had been trying to get that damned ball back to the exact same point it had started from. Every evening for two fucking months, he had been made fun of by all his friends because all he ever did was make one break shot after another, like an idiot, senselessly, hour after hour. One evening, Lorenzo had even come and asked him what was going through his head.

"Go away," Dino had said. He felt strong, almost one of the elect, someone who was fighting for something absurd but greater than himself.

"But what are you doing?" Lorenzo had asked with a frown. "Have you gone mad or something? Come and have a game."

"Go away," Dino had said again, shooting yet another ball from the opening position. The ball had bounced off the cushion and ended up a few centimetres from where it had started.

"Shit," Dino had said between his teeth, jerking his head forward slightly.

Lorenzo had watched him for another moment or two as he bent to make another break shot.

"OK," Lorenzo had said. "Do what you like." And as he went back to his friends, he had made a gesture to them that meant Dino must be completely crazy.

And for what? Why, for two whole months, had he looked like someone who'd gone soft in the head? That was something he had asked himself more than once during all that time, and the only thing that came into his mind was Cirillo's cue, that way he had of cradling it and kissing the ball with it. He knew he had to succeed in getting the ball back to the exact same point from which it had started. That had been something greater than him, something wider and thicker, something Dino couldn't really decipher, let alone understand, but it was a tremor that rose up like a fountain from somewhere inside his stomach. Many years later, a bookseller would give Dino a funny little book of Japanese stories in which young monks, for no very clear reason, were struck by some reply their master gave them, and from that moment their lives were illuminated with a new light. Dino had found it rather an irritating book and had wondered why that funny little bookseller with the protruding ears had given it to him. But then he had remembered that moment when, as a young man himself, he had succeeded for the first time in getting the ball back to the exact same place from which it had started, and he had wondered if it was basically the same thing that those young Japanese monks had felt. In fact, for a few minutes, from the moment the ball had stopped as if by magic in the same spot from which it had started, until the moment Cirillo had stood up and smashed everything into millions of fragments with that terrible "Every time?", Dino had entered an unknown region of the world, illuminated by a new, clearer light, in which things seemed to fit perfectly and to be made of some strange crystalline material. It had been a moment when the world had really seemed to have a meaning, be less distant, however incomprehensible.

But then everything had come crashing down, and Cirillo's hammer blow had made that crystalline patina explode into millions of pieces, and the world had gone back to being the way it always had been—dirty and stinking and heavy as lead, only now even heavier than ever, with sacks of sand hanging on all sides like ballast.

Every time. There was a terrifying feeling of eternity about those simple words, capable of cutting off the strongest man at the knees. Every time. Dino had been practising for two months, two horrible, ridiculous, agonising months, and in all that time the ball had only ever returned once to its exact opening position, and now that he thought about it there was a strong possibility that had been a stroke of luck. How long would it take him to succeed every time? As he walked home with tears starting to well up in his eyes, disconsolately kicking a piece of cardboard, Dino had seen himself as an old, grey-haired man, bent over a billiard table with his back broken and his legs shaky, still playing break shots, one after the other, like a halfwit. The funny thing was, and he couldn't quite figure out why, he had also seen a whole lot of people gathered round that table and that old man, watching his every move almost admiringly. But in the end he hadn't paid much attention to that—all he had seen had been that infinite expanse of hours spent making break shots, one after the other, like a moron.

That evening, when he had got back home, he had gone straight to his room, saying that he felt sick and didn't want anything to eat. He had stayed awake until dawn, convinced that it was pointless, that he would never succeed, that there wasn't any sense in playing billiards at all, and, trying to imagine what life would be like without the music of those balls hitting each other or those perfect geometries that seemed to put things in their rightful place, he had finally fallen asleep.

In the morning, he had gone to work with his father, and had spent that day, as always, fitting stones into the earth, and for every stone that he hammered into the sand he told himself that this would be his life—laying stones, one after the other, millions of stones, until he grew old. He would pave his own life with stones, and that endless road towards old age suddenly didn't even seem so terrible, tempered by that inevitability which, all things considered, even seems to set the world straight. By the time he had taken off his overalls in the evening and Giorgone had asked him why he had been so quiet all day and he had answered with a shrug of the shoulders, he had become almost serenely resigned to that life. He had thought of himself as some kind of honest modern hero, the hero of little things, with a dignity and an honour that might not be so showy but was no less noble. He had set off for home, then turned right onto the street that led to the river, which they had only recently finished paving, come to the entrance to the billiard parlour, gone downstairs to the tables, taken off his jacket, got the balls out of the little drawer, taken a cue from the wall, stroked it with the chalk, leant across the table and, thinking about that road covered in stones that would take him a long way, played a break shot in which the ball had ended up quite some distance from where it had started.

One evening a few months later, as it was getting towards closing time and Dino had already decided that he didn't really much want to go home, there had been a little incident. Everyone had gone home, and Cirillo was having a last, relaxed game with a guy called Gigetto Aspirina. All at once, there had been a kind of explosion on the other side of the room. Cirillo and Gigetto Aspirina had stepped quickly away from the table to see what was happening. At the table right at the back of the room Dino was standing holding the cue tightly in both hands and hacking away with it, hitting the wall and the nearby tables, cursing all the saints and Madonnas he could think of, smashing the cue into a shower of fragments.

"What the hell!" Gigetto had yelled.

Gigetto Aspirina wasn't the kind of person you wanted to cross—even though some of the rumours about him might have been far-fetched, his tiny body was capable of a surprising strength and aggressiveness, which had more than once landed him in prison.

Without taking his eyes off Dino, who was still smashing the cue and cursing back there at the far end of the room, Cirillo had put a hand in front of Gigetto. "Stop," he had said.

Gigetto had looked Cirillo up and down, angry and puzzled. "The guy's destroying everything, boss."

"Let him be," Cirillo had said.

After a while, Dino had slowed down, until he had stopped completely and dropped what was left of the cue and collapsed on the floor and started sobbing, propped up against one leg of the table with his hands over his eyes.

"What a pansy," Gigetto had said.

Cirillo had looked at Dino for a few moments without moving, then had gone back to his table, put his cue down and taken a bunch of keys from his pocket. He had chosen one and stretched up towards one of the display cases hanging on the wall. He had stood there for a few seconds, looking at the cues in the case, then reached out his hand and taken out a colourful wooden one with little diamond-shaped inlays. He had closed the case again, put the keys back in his pocket, and with the cue in his hand walked calmly across the room.

When he had come level with Dino's table, the boy was still there, sobbing, hunched over like a wet pine cone next to a leg of the table.

"Here," Cirillo had said. "Try this one."

Dino had opened his swollen eyes for a moment and sniffed for the umpteenth time. Standing in front of him, as straight as an officer, with no expression in his eyes that could be made out, there was Cirillo, and next to him, held firmly like a halberd, a colourful, shiny cue.

"What?" Dino had said, his voice still half-cracked.

"I said try this," Cirillo had said.

Dino had looked at Cirillo again, then again at the cue, and after a few seconds, sniffing a few more times, he had got to his feet.

"It's an Arlecchino," Dino had said.

"I know it's an Arlecchino," Cirillo had said.

"They don't make them any more," Dino had said.

"I know they don't make them any more," Cirillo had said. "Take it."

Timidly, Dino had held out his hand and taken hold of the cue. He had never held a cue like that before. It felt warm and alive, it felt as if it had been made by God himself, and for a moment Dino had wondered if there was a special knack to using it.

"Is it mine?" Dino had asked, looking again at Cirillo for a moment, with the hint of a smile coming back into his eyes.

"Like fuck it is," Cirillo had said, and, throwing a last glance at his cue and at the boy, he had turned and started back towards his table. After a couple of steps he had stopped and turned and looked Dino straight in the eyes.

"And if you break this one," he had said, "I'll break your legs."

One evening a few months later, at least a year and a half since Dino had succeeded in getting the ball to come back to its starting point, at a time when there were still a few people playing here and there, Cirillo had walked up to Dino's table.

"How long is it since you last made a bad shot?" Cirillo had asked.

Dino was already leaning across the table, ready for another shot. He turned his head for a moment and stared at Cirillo for a few seconds. "Three days," he had said as he straightened up in front of Cirillo, holding the Arlecchino in front of his chest with both hands. He seemed to have got older, and in his eyes there was that mixture of courage and sadness which Cirillo had seen, many years earlier, in the eyes of soldiers coming back from the front.

For a moment longer, Cirillo had continued looking that strange boy in the eyes, then he had taken a cigarette, put it in his mouth, lit it, taken a drag, and as he blew out the smoke tapped the cigarette lighter a few times on the edge of the table, then given a little laugh and taken another rapid glance at Dino. When this whole thing had started, he would have bet anything against him. To get the ball back to the exact same position from which it had started, and to do it every time—it was absurd, it was impossible, no one could do it. Even if they had tried, no one would be so crazy, so moronic, as to continue trying day after day. And if they hadn't been mad when they started, they would certainly have gone mad as they went along, playing one break shot after another.

When, that day almost two years earlier, the boy had come up to his table and disturbed him, Cirillo had felt a kind of shock. But—and this was perhaps even more surprising—he hadn't lost his temper. Anyone else who had disturbed Cirillo as he was playing, worse still, just as he was about to shoot—even thinking about it was like blasphemy—would, in the best of cases, have looked at like a madman, told in no uncertain terms to go away, and finally been given a thrashing he wouldn't forget in a hurry. Instead of which, for some reason it had seemed almost normal that this boy should interrupt his game—and his life—like that, and instead of his losing his temper, a kind of summer calm had descended on Cirillo. Of course, he had no intention of giving lessons—he had never taken any and he didn't believe in them and would never give them. Billiards was a battlefield, in which every trajectory intersected until they formed the thickest of forests, so thick that you didn't know how to get out of it or how to defend yourself, but in which you had to find the direction by yourself. Billiards was a matter of muscles and heart, and you had to learn for yourself how to take the blows and get out alive. That was Cirillo's billiards, a world of stinking parlours and dirty baize, money laid on the edge of the table, sometimes binges after a game, hunger and pains in the stomach when you lost your bearings—until that magical evening fifteen years earlier, when he had beaten two-thirds of the room with a perfect shot, hitting two cushions, then knocking his opponent's ball straight into the castle. Those who were present still remembered that game between Cirillo and the Baron, still talked about it with that gleam in their eyes that people get when they've seen something that can't really be put into words.

"Let's do something," Cirillo had said, still tapping the silver cigarette lighter on the edge of the table. "I don't give lessons, I don't believe in them. But if you like we can play together. Whenever you like. Maybe tomorrow."

"OK," Dino had said, and inside him there were thirty or forty people crying in every corner of his body.

"See you tomorrow, then," Cirillo had said, a half-smile hovering over his lips.

"See you tomorrow."

Cirillo had tapped the cigarette lighter on the table a couple more times, more loudly, then had turned and started walking back to his own table.

"What about this?"

Cirillo had stopped and turned to look back at Dino, who had bent the Arlecchino slightly to one side, as if to show it.

"You can carry on using it, if you like," Cirillo had said. "And if you manage to beat me it's yours."

Chapter Nine

D INO DIDN'T REALLY KNOW where to go, or even how
to go back to his friends, who were still laying those round
pieces of stone that had started to look more like corpses. That
was how Dino saw himself and his workmates now—grave-
diggers dressed in black, moving like automata, throwing down
corpses of stone, pale and tired and travelling along an avenue
that led to darkness. That day everything ended in darkness, in
that filthy, sticky black sludge that Dino had seen for the first
time when he had gone to visit his cousin who was ill.

"Hi," Dino had said when he had got to the hospital and
was at his cousin's bedside.

"Hi," his cousin had said, in a thin voice.

"So how are you?" Dino had asked, as if everything was
normal. There were tubes in his cousin's nose and arms, and
a funny machine with a strange coloured thing that passed
behind a dark pane of glass and every now and again made
a weird noise.

.“I'm dying,” Dino's cousin had said, with a smile and a shrug, his voice not much more than a breath.

Dino had nodded, and for a moment he, too, had smiled. “It happens,” he had said.

This cousin had often met up with Dino in the centre of town, and they had all gone around in a group, boys and girls, and Dino had shown him a good time.

“Yes, it happens,” his cousin had sighed, trying to laugh a bit.

For a few moments, the two of them had fallen silent, while the machine kept making that strange sound, beating time.

“Listen,” Dino had said after a while, “what is all that stuff on the roads?”

“What stuff?” Dino's cousin had sighed again, then he had had a little coughing fit, making the bed squeak.

“I don't know,” Dino had said. “It's black.”

His cousin had raised his eyebrows a little, slightly bewildered, and looked at Dino. “It's asphalt,” he had said after a while, and sighed.

Dino had looked at him gravely for a few seconds, as if all at once that stuff had come into the room, or as if it had been that stuff that had seeped into his cousin's bones and dragged him onto that deathbed.

“Shit,” Dino had said looking his cousin straight in the eyes.

When Dino got to the site, the others were working as usual. Duilio and Blondie were on their knees on the ground, laying the stones in the damp base, while some distance away Saeed was watering the ground with a long tube attached to the pump of the old tanker truck. From time to time, Duilio would look up to see what Blondie was doing and sometimes, saying "Hey" or giving him a blow with the end of the little hammer if he was closer, would tell him to straighten the stones or not to turn them so much. It was quite annoying, as Dino must surely know, but in the end, with no little effort, even Blondie had learnt to bear it. Above all, he had learnt that most of the time, for reasons he didn't entirely understand, Duilio was right.

Saeed, on the other hand, would from time to time spurt a little water in Duilio's direction and grin. "HEY!" Duilio would yell, jerking backwards. This was something that Dino had done when he was younger, on sunny days. It was odd—it was as if this whole business of putting the stones down on the road carried with it a whole world of gestures and habits that each person had to learn for himself. The funny thing was then to continue spurting some water at Duilio, and watch him yell "HEY!" every time like a caveman, and make that sudden movement with his back, but the best thing of all, after at least six or seven of these *heys*, was to see the tiny, elderly figure of Duilio all at once, at the umpteenth spurt, jump to his feet with surprising agility and yell, red in the face, "HEEYY! I'll stick that tube up your arse, got that? Son of a bitch!" Then, with the same speed with which he had leapt to his feet, he would crouch down again and resume work as if nothing had happened. And the nice thing was that none of the anger in that outburst lasted any time at all—as soon as he was back at work he became the same polite, taciturn Duilio as ever, as if he didn't even remember what had happened.

Dino came level with his workmates. Saeed spurted some more water in Duilio's direction, and Duilio gave his usual backwards jerk and yelled his usual "HEY!" Blondie looked up at Saeed and they smiled at each other, then turned towards Dino.

"Hello, boys," Dino said, also trying to smile. "I have to talk to you for a minute."

Saeed and Blondie didn't quite know how to interpret that not very convincing half-smile, or the fact that Dino hadn't taken his hands out of his jacket, but Duilio had known immediately that something was wrong. He knew Dino too well not to recognise in his eyes when something bad was brewing. He had seen him playing when he was a little boy, he had seen him laying his first stones together with his father. He had seen him laugh and cry, and none of the nuances in between held much of a secret for him any more.

"What's happened, son?" Duilio asked.

"It's better if we go over there," Dino said.

Saeed shut off the tap controlling the water then went to turn off the pump on the tanker truck, while Blondie helped Duilio to his feet.

"Getting older," Duilio said.

They all went up on the pavement and took up positions, leaning on a lamp post, perching on the edge of the barrow or sitting on sacks of earth. They all looked at Dino, who continued standing there with his hands in his pockets and that weary half-smile on his face.

Dino glanced at them and then kicked a little stone. "They're going to use asphalt," he said, looking the other three in the eyes.

Saeed, Duilio and Blondie looked at each other uncomprehendingly.

"What?" Duilio said.

"THEY'RE GOING TO USE ASPHALT!" Dino said, raising his voice. "They're going to use asphalt," he said again, kicking another little stone.

"Asphalt?" Duilio said with a frown.

"Yes, asphalt," Dino said, nodding, his chin jutting out, his hands spreading in the pockets of his jacket.

"What means, 'They're going to use asphalt'?" Saeed said.

"It means the town council have decided there's no more money, so they're going to use asphalt to surface the streets."

"What about stones?" Blondie asked, in that strange hard foreign accent of his.

"No more stones, Blondie. They'll be covered over with asphalt."

"But is not possible!" Blondie said.

"Yes, it is," Dino said. "It's possible."

Saeed took a step back and kicked the lamp post. "Fuck," he said.

All four of them were silent for a while, each staring ahead of him at a different spot, looking for roads that stretched away in unknown directions.

"What about us?" Saeed asked after a while.

Dino raised his eyes and looked straight at Saeed. "Each of us can do what he likes," he said. "I hired you to lay stones, but the council hired you to surface the streets. Those who want to can stay and learn how to lay asphalt, those who don't want to can go, and nobody will make any fuss." He was silent for a moment longer, while the others all glanced at him in turn. "As far as I'm concerned, you don't even have to finish this street."

Duilio raised his head abruptly. "Are you crazy?" he said. "The street has to be finished, fuck it, even if it's the last street I do. And fuck asphalt."

The others laughed and then, as if everything was normal, they all went back to work.

When Dino got home that evening, Sofia knew immediately that something had happened. Dino had that look in his eyes of someone who has seen a world that will no longer be the same, and still doesn't quite know which way to turn. He had not even gone to the billiard parlour and, instead of blue chalk marks, his hands still bore the marks of earth and work.

"Have you been working all this time?" Sofia asked him from the kitchen, with a ladle in her hand.

"No, I went for a walk," Dino said, hanging his jacket on the coat stand and coming towards Sofia.

"Hi," he said, planting a kiss on her lips and a hand on her belly. "How's he doing?" Then he turned and took something from one of the shelves in the kitchen.

Sofia grabbed him by a corner of his sleeve. "Come here," she said. "What's the matter?" She pulled him to her, trying in vain to get him to look her in the eyes.

"Nothing, don't worry," Dino said, trying to smile. "Everything will be all right, you'll see." He kissed Sofia on the forehead and turned away. He opened a cabinet, took a glass, filled it with water and drank it all in one go. Then he placed his hands on the shelf of the cabinet and stood there like that, his face to the wall and his head half-bowed.

Sofia again took a few steps towards him and placed a hand on his back. "What's the matter?" she asked in a low voice.

Dino heaved a deep sigh and raised his head slightly. "They're going to use asphalt," he said, still with his back to her, then after a few seconds he turned. His eyes were swollen with something he couldn't find his way out of. "No more stones."

Sofia moved closer and slipped into his arms. "I'm sorry," she said.

Chapter Ten

DINO AND SOFIA were still in the middle of their dinner when they heard knocking at the door. Puzzled, they stopped and looked at each other.

Dino frowned, put his fork down on his plate and wiped his mouth with a napkin and got up and went to open the door. Outside stood Duilio, wearing a pair of greyish trousers, an old brown velvet jacket a little bit too big for him and a green felt hat that was different from the one he usually wore to work.

"Oh," Dino said. "Duilio."

"Hi, son, can I come in?" Duilio asked, with a slightly sad look on his face.

"Of course," Dino said, and opened the door wide.

"Thanks," Duilio said, lowering his head as he came in.

When he was inside and saw Sofia sitting at the table with a half-full plate in front of her, he gave a little start, quickly took off his hat and threw Dino an embarrassed look. "Oh, you're still eating," he said. "I'm sorry. I'll come back later. Or maybe tomorrow."

"Don't worry," Dino said, closing the door and going back to his seat. "No problem. Would you like something?"

"No, thanks," Duilio said. "I've already eaten."

Dino had picked up his fork and plunged it in his food. "Sit down," he said, indicating one of the other chairs with his chin, then reached out and filled an unused glass with wine.

"Thanks," Duilio said, nodding, then stepped forward to the chair, holding his hat in front of his chest with both hands. He put his hat to one side and sat down, still looking as tense as when he had come in. "Good evening, Sofia," he said, bowing his head again slightly in greeting.

"Hi, Duilio," Sofia smiled, before plunging her fork back into her food.

Dino pushed the glass of wine towards Duilio, then took a sip of his own.

"You eat late," Duilio said, picking up the glass with thumb and finger and raising it to his mouth.

It was funny seeing Duilio outside work, it was like suddenly realising that he was a man, too, an old man just as shy and embarrassed as anyone else, not that rough beast of burden who was quite capable of spending all day bent over the road without uttering a single word.

"Sofia usually waits for me to come back from the billiard parlour," Dino said, shoving a forkful of food in his mouth.

"Oh, yes, the billiard parlour," Duilio said, nodding and trying for a moment to throw Sofia a slight smile.

Sofia also tried to give a little smile, then for a while all three were silent, Dino and Sofia wiping their plates with hunks of bread and Duilio sipping at his wine.

"What's the matter, Duilio?" Dino asked. "Would you prefer it if we were alone?"

Duilio glanced at Sofia and thought for a moment that it might not be a bad idea, then realised that it didn't really matter. "I'm quitting, son," he said.

Dino and Sofia raised their eyes from their plates and looked at Duilio in surprise, then Dino nodded, which seemed the most natural thing to do.

As Sofia put the plates in the kitchen sink, she glanced back at the two men. For a moment, a strange mixture of anger and sadness welled up inside her, and she would have given part of herself to help those two men who were trying to come to terms with something that was greater than them. Then she told herself that perhaps it was the baby, and she stopped thinking about it.

"I've been laying stones for forty years," Duilio said, "first with your poor dad, now with you. You know that. I should have retired before now, but working on the streets kept me company. Not like this, though. I can't bear to see that black stuff covering everything. I don't want anything to do with that shit." He looked up for a moment at Sofia and raised one hand a little. "Sorry, Sofia."

"That's all right," Sofia said from the kitchenette, giving a slight smile. Dino, still looking at Duilio, ate a piece of bread and sipped his wine.

"I went to see Giani," Duilio went on, looking at Dino again, then down at the table. "I asked him how much they owed me if I quit. He told me to wait a minute and went to have a quick word with his secretary, then he came back inside holding a little piece of paper with something scribbled on it. He told me they were rough figures, that it would take a while to make exact accounts and anyway it wasn't up to them. But he gave me an idea. It wasn't such a small amount, son. Not huge, but not that small either. I can get by easily enough. Plus, I've put a bit aside, and who knows, maybe with the severance pay and the money I can get if I sell my place here in town, I can buy something out of town, in the country. Rita would be happy. Maybe I could get hold of a bit of land and turn it into a vegetable garden. Rita might like a few animals, too. I didn't think I'd ever leave town, I prefer stone to earth. But now … "

He tailed off, his words hanging in mid-air like little balls that he couldn't get hold of again.

"Yes I know," Dino said rolling a piece of soft bread into a ball.

The two men sat in silence for a while, while behind them Sofia dried the dishes. Dino threw his head back slightly.

"Do you need a hand?" he asked.

Sofia glanced at him and finished drying the bowl. "I've almost finished," she said.

For a few more seconds, Dino sat half-turned towards Sofia, then he turned and looked down at the table again, then up at Duilio.

"Saeed's going, too," he said.

"Yes, I know," Duilio said.

"He's going back to bricklaying."

"Yes, he told me."

"He's doing the right thing."

"Yes, he's doing the right thing," Duilio said, taking another sip of wine.

A few days earlier, Saeed had gone up to Dino as they were working and asked him if they could talk for a moment. He had told him that some time earlier he had met his old foreman, who had recently started his own construction company and needed a bricklayer.

"I say no at first. Tell him I got good job with good people. But now … I want to work with stone and earth, not sticky black stuff like devil's sick."

Dino had put one hand over the other and looked into Saeed's sad eyes. "You're doing the right thing, Saeed. Don't worry."

Then they had gone back to work, and every stone had seemed to weigh a few more kilos than usual.

"I'm sorry," Duilio said, and took a last sip from his glass.

Dino looked up at that old man he had seen laying stones for as long as he could remember. He stared at him for a while, trying to hold back the memories. "What for?" he said. "You're doing the right thing, Duilio. I'd do the same if I could. It's just that I don't know anything else. Plus, there's the baby on the way. What can I do?"

"I know, son," Duilio said. "Don't worry. Things will work out, you'll see." With a bit of difficulty, he rose from the chair.

Dino nodded to himself, staring at his two hands as they played with the soft piece of bread.

"I'm off," Duilio said, again holding the hat with both hands. "It's getting late."

Dino looked up at Duilio, as if surprised, and after a moment got to his feet. Duilio waved goodbye to Sofia, then let Dino walk him to the door. They hugged, then Duilio looked Dino straight in the eyes and smiled slightly and gave him a pat on the cheek.

"Cheer up, son," Duilio said. "And try to stay well."

"Yes, you too," Dino said, and watched as Duilio put his hat back on with both hands and walked away, his back stooped, down the dimly lit corridor.

Chapter Eleven

T HAT VILE BEAST APPEARED at the end of the street, puffing and shaking. A gigantic mouth full of black steaming sludge gaped open, as if stupefied, with pieces of tar dripping from it like some demonic slime. As the beast advanced, it was as if someone was twisting its guts with a pair of pliers, making it creak and groan with pain, forcing it to squeeze out into the sky that smoke as dense and black as effluent from the sewers. As it came closer, it gradually slowed down and sank into itself, hissing and blowing white steam from its ears. It gave a final belch, and a lump of black sludge rolled down one side of its foaming mouth and settled on the rest of the steaming heap.

Dino and Blondie were standing side by side, wearing those embarrassing blue uniforms which made them look like puppets. Next to them stood a man as broad as a chest of drawers, with a rust-red beard and hair and two swollen hands that looked harder than anvils, also wearing that ungainly blue uniform. He had a flat nose that looked as if someone had squashed it, and his eyes were slightly narrow, as if someone was pulling them from the sides.

"That's Molly," the red-haired man said, his mouth turning up slightly in a smile.

Blondie turned and looked for a moment at the red-haired man with barely concealed disgust, then spat on the ground and again looked straight ahead. "Shit," he said.

The vile beast gave one last jolt, shaking itself thoroughly, then all at once went to sleep, and all that was left in the air was the smoke from its slime and the harsh, nauseating miasma that hit you in the nose and turned your stomach.

From the back of the beast, a thin, curly-haired man emerged and slowly walked down a little flight of steps to street level.

"That's Carlo," the red-haired man said, watching as the other man reached the ground and started towards them. "He's in charge of Molly."

The thin, curly-haired man gave the beast a last satisfied look as he passed it, and even moved his hand over it. "Well?" he said, almost yelling, as he approached, looking back contentedly at the beast. "How do you like my baby?"

Dino and Blondie looked again at that foul monster and that fetid mouth and that steaming black sludge and those lumps of tar.

"Well ... " Dino said.

Blondie looked at Carlo as if he wanted to punch him, but said nothing.

"Hi, I'm Carlo," Carlo said when he was level with them, smiling and holding out his hand.

"I'm Dino," Dino said.

Blondie held out his hand, but only that—he didn't say a word.

Carlo looked up at the sky. A few snow-white clouds were peeping out from behind the roofs, making the sky bluer than usual. "Lovely day," he said, putting his hands on his hips and breathing in great mouthfuls of air. "Smell that air," he said.

Dino and Blondie exchanged surprised glances, wondering if he was pulling their legs.

"Well, now," Carlo said, turning back to look at them. "They say you've never laid asphalt before. Is that right?"

Dino and Blondie nodded without saying a word.

"It's a walk in the park, you'll see. Molly tips the asphalt onto the road. We just have to spread it as smoothly as we can, then we go over it a few times with the roller and it's all done. A bit different from those bloody stones, isn't it?" He gave Dino a pat on the shoulder and winked.

Dino looked at his shoulder as if something had got stuck to it, then looked at Carlo and put a hand in front of Blondie, who had already sprung forward like an animal.

"Hey," Carlo said, taking a step back, still smiling. "Me and you best friends. OK?"

The red-haired man took a step back from Dino and Blondie. "What's the matter?" he asked, looking gravely at Blondie, who couldn't somehow get his jaw to slacken.

"It's all right," Dino said to the red-haired man, but without taking his hand off Blondie's chest. "It's been a long few days." He turned, looked Blondie straight in the eyes and forced him to calm down.

"It's nice to know I'll be working with good people," Carlo said, rubbing his hands. "All right," he went on as he turned and went back towards the beast. "Go and get the shovels from behind Molly. As soon as the roller gets here we'll start."

Blondie and the red-haired man looked each other in the eyes for a few seconds, then both spat on the ground and walked with Dino towards the beast.

As it turned out, the red-haired man wasn't such a bad guy. He called himself Johnny. Apparently a friend of his had started calling him that one day because, he said, he looked like a foreign biker, and the name had stuck.

"Nothing wrong with it," Johnny had said, tearing off a large piece from his roll.

"No," Dino had said, with a half-laugh. "Nothing wrong with it."

Blondie had not said anything, although his jaw had been almost completely relaxed for a few days now.

Dino's days were enlivened by Johnny's curses and Carlo's jokes, then in the evening after work, as usual, he went to the billiard parlour to lose his game with Cirillo, who would watch him with a slightly puzzled look on his face, from the other side of the table.

Later, after dinner, Dino would stretch out on the sofa or the bed with Sofia. It was nice to see his wife's belly grow like a dome from day to day. He had learnt to love that hemisphere of flesh, like a hill where, or so it seemed to him, all the roads he couldn't find any more in his dreams somehow met.

All in all, things seemed almost normal, and those curses, those jokes, those games and above all that dome on Sofia's belly seemed almost to give a meaning to days spent endlessly spreading that putrid black sticky sludge that assaulted your nose.

It's a strange thing, but in the end man is a malleable animal, and somehow adapts, however reluctantly, to the roughest of surfaces, just as, day by day, that black cancer swallowed up the unknown order of the stones.

At first, Dino had thought he would never get used to it. As that first small load of steaming black bitumen descended on his stones and swallowed them like death, it had seemed to him as if the world as he had known it until then had come to an end. At the very moment when that that black muck had touched the ground, a solid, stinking lump had come away from Dino's throat and had slid slowly, with a lot of pain and retching, deep down into his stomach and had filled him with a nausea which he knew, even though he had only had the merest hint of it so far, would never go away again. And in that same moment, a crack had appeared, and something in the mechanism of his life had jammed. He was alive, he was surviving, but none of the things that had kept him going were working the way they had. There was no more air to breathe, there were no more dreams or systems of universes or roads with an incomprehensible order that led to fantastic or extraordinary places, there was only a uniform, all-pervading, necrotic expanse of black sludge which made everything disappear in the flash of an eye.

And yet, like a steam engine with hidden pistons and pumps, Dino had, to his own surprise, managed to keep going despite everything.

Chapter Twelve

TALKING ABOUT IT LATER, some people were willing to swear they had actually heard the blast. Maybe because when these things happen everybody wants to grab a bit of the limelight, as if for a few moments they feel they somehow must play a role.

Cirillo had had a few things to sort out with Sandro, and had told Dino to go to the table in the meantime and take out the cue, and he would be with him soon.

"OK," Dino had said. "I'd like to shoot a few balls for myself anyway."

Cirillo had nodded, and Dino had walked as usual towards the far end of the room, calmly taken off his sweater, and rolled up his shirtsleeves, and as he was starting to bend his left wrist towards his elbow his eye had fallen on a small bitumen stain on the back of his thumb. He scratched it with the nail of his fourth finger and saw it clear slightly, then raised his hand to his nose and sniffed. For a moment, he

97

was again overwhelmed by the smell that surrounded him all day, that hot sour smell of tar, which seemed to stick to him like flypaper. He had washed his hands five times after work, but those damned tar stains just wouldn't go away. He finished rolling up his shirtsleeve and walked to the display case next to the table, opened it, took out the Arlecchino, took a piece of chalk from the edge of the table, rubbed it between his forefinger and his thumb and then gave a few little strokes to the tip of the cue. Then he turned towards the table—some of the pins were down, but Dino didn't take any notice. He placed the point of the cue on the white ball, hit it, then picked it up with two fingers and dropped it into his T-shirt, which he was holding out with his other hand, cleaned it properly and put it back on the table. He lifted the cue and again placed the tip of it against the ball and pushed the ball until it was more or less in the middle of his part of the table. He then leant over the table, made a bridge with his fingers, placed the cue over it and, moving the wrist of his right hand slightly from side to side, calmly sized up the shot. Then he let his arm go and the cue hit the ball, which rolled calmly towards the opposite cushion, rebounded off it and came back to the spot from which it had started. Dino was still leaning over the green baize, as if he had not yet made the shot, and watched the ball closely as it returned to its position. Usually when he was in a good mood, this was the moment when he smiled. It always created a certain impression, seeing the ball come back to its original position, it was as if, all at once, things fitted into place, as if despite everything there was a free zone in which things found their true level. But that evening, he didn't feel like smiling. In fact, when he saw the ball come back to its place, he felt a strange sense of unease which he couldn't quite pin down.

He did not move and for a few seconds looked at the ball sitting there, motionless, in front of the tip of his cue, then again started moving the wrist of his right hand and, as naturally as ever, let the cue go until it hit the ball, which as usual rolled towards the opposite cushion and came back to the point from which it had started. Again, Dino stood motionless, looking at the ball as it sat there, also motionless, a few centimetres from the tip of his cue, then as if something didn't feel right he tilted his head slightly to one side and gave a little frown.

It was at that moment that a cry echoed through the room. "They planted a bomb in the town hall!"

Dino turned his head abruptly towards the entrance—Rafferto, whose father owned the cold-meat shop, was on the stairs, leaning down, probably holding himself on the banisters, with a kind of amused half-smile in his eyes.

"They planted a what?" someone cried, running towards the exit.

"A bomb!" Rafferto replied, already disappearing up the stairs.

Dino and someone who was playing at the next table got to their feet and looked at each other, frowning slightly, then, without putting down their cues, started walking towards the back of the room.

Four or five of them ended up standing out in the street, at the entrance to the billiard parlour. A few people were passing as if nothing had happened, while others were walking quickly or even running in the direction of the town hall. Dino and Cirillo looked at each other and frowned. For some reason, Dino thought that it was strange to be out here with his cue in his hand, as if they were inseparable.

After a few minutes, Marcello, the shoemaker, went by in the opposite direction.

"Hey!" Cirillo cried.

"Hi," Marcello said.

"Well?"

"You mean the town hall?"

"Yes," Cirillo said.

Marcello shrugged and gave a little laugh. "Nothing much," he said. "A couple of broken windows. We did more damage throwing stones when we were kids."

Cirillo and Dino both laughed.

"But was it really a bomb?" Cirillo cried.

Marcello, who had already moved on a bit, turned for a moment. "So they say," he replied, walking backwards for a few steps. Then he raised his hand to wave goodbye and continued on his way.

Dino and Cirillo also raised their arms, then looked at each other again and shrugged their shoulders as Marcello had done, and after a minute or two went back into the billiard parlour and carried on with their game.

Chapter Thirteen

I T HAD NOW BEEN several months since Dino and Blondie had stopped laying stones in the ground and started swimming in those rivers of black sludge. Dino, Johnny and Blondie were sitting calmly at a table in a café with glasses in front of them, watching the people passing, with the top half of their uniforms tied around their waists and the vague impression of being on holiday.

Blondie would never remember how they had ended up talking about that, nor perhaps, if he had thought about it, would Dino. It was one of those conversations you have as you watch people passing by, full of pauses and clichés, things that are said and then forgotten. But they would never forget the way Johnny laughed, especially Dino. That laugh seemed to come from another world, or directly from hell, and it hit that little café table like a rock. For a moment, it even seemed to Dino and Blondie that Johnny's face had been twisted into the shape of some unknown animal's.

"Who told you that crap?" Johnny said to Dino, laughing, his face still twisted in a kind of grimace.

Dino looked at Johnny and put his glass down on the table. "Giani did," Dino said, almost under his breath.

Johnny gave another of those laughs that seemed to come from another world, and for a moment he actually threw his head back, then turned to look at Dino and Blondie again, his eyes watery from the laughter.

"Well, friend," Johnny said. "Either Giani is dumber than you or he told you a load of crap hoping you'd swallow it. It was a kickback, Dino."

Dino looked at Blondie with a grave, perplexed expression, that corrosive substance gradually spreading like acid through his body.

"A kickback?" Dino asked, frowning and leaning forward in his chair.

Johnny looked at Dino with an amused smile, and for a moment he had the feeling that Blondie understood. "Do you really think," he said, "that resurfacing all the streets costs that much less than having you guys lay stones?"

Dino continued staring at Johnny without saying anything, motionless on his chair with one hand on his glass, like a lump of granite.

"I'm sorry," Johnny went on, looking him in the eyes and still smiling, "but do you really think the whole town needs resurfacing? Outside the centre, maybe, on the ring roads.

It might be useful there. Or else out on those empty streets where all the new building work is going on. But think about it. Do you really believe they'd award a contract to resurface everything, just like that, overnight?"

Johnny took a last sip from his glass and again looked at Dino, who hadn't taken his eyes off him.

"Well, who knows?" he said, shaking his head slightly, an amused expression on his face, as if he were talking to a little boy. He wiped his mouth with a napkin, using both hands to do so, and laughed. "Maybe that's why someone planted a bomb."

Dino stared at him for a few more seconds, then got abruptly to his feet, making the glasses on the table clink and strode off down the street.

"What about the bill?" Johnny shouted after him, laughing as he watched Dino disappear round the corner.

When he looked back at the table, Blondie was still staring at him.

"Blondie," Johnny said, smiling, "just stay calm, it wasn't anything to do with me."

When Dino came into the office, Giani was sitting comfortably in his armchair, talking on the phone with an amused look on his face. Dino slammed the door behind him, walked straight up to Giani's desk, leant forward, grabbed the receiver, tore it from Giani's ear, much to his astonishment,

105

slammed it down with all his might, put both his hands flat on the desk and snarled, "Why are you resurfacing the whole town?"

"Dino, are you crazy? What's the fuck's got into you?"

"Why are you resurfacing the whole town?" Dino said again, raising his voice even more.

"Hey!" Giani yelled in his face. "Get away from this desk and calm down!"

The two men looked each other in the eyes, and for a moment Giani thought Dino was going to hit him.

"Shit!" Dino cried, straightening up suddenly and going to the window.

"Christ, Dino, what's got into you?"

"Tell me why you're resurfacing the whole town," Dino said, staring at a clump of bushes in the yard outside.

"What's the matter with you? I already told you. The council did their sums and decided that's what they were going to do."

A big pigeon landed near the tall pine in the middle of the yard, pecked at something on the gravel and flew away again.

"It was a kickback, wasn't it?" Dino said, without even turning round.

"A kickback?" Giani said, frowning.

"Yes, a kickback."

"What are you talking about?"

Dino lowered his head a little to get a better look at the grey clouds which had appeared from behind the roofs and didn't look too promising, then turned again towards Giani and leant back against the window pane, his hands and his backside on the sill.

"Why are they resurfacing the whole town, instead of doing one part first? Why all of a sudden? Why now, when there's a new councillor? Why specifically here, where there've always been stones?"

Dino asked all these questions in a calm voice, without taking his eyes off Giani's eyes, like a soldier demanding to know from his superior officer why they are sending him on a suicide mission.

For a few seconds, Giani sat there, grave and silent, without taking his eyes off Dino, it seemed to both of them that, in some way, they had never been so close.

"I don't know," Giani said, as sharp and hard as a rock. "It's none of my business. And it's none of your business either. We're not here to ask questions, Dino, we're here to do what they tell us to do. Those are the rules of the game."

For a while, all Dino could hear was his own breathing and the beating of his heart, then the inside of his lips swelled and a little air escaped. The two men looked at each other a few seconds longer, watching resignedly as a wall rose between them, then Dino nodded and without saying a word left the room and closed the door behind him.

For as long as he could, Giani watched Dino walk slowly away down the corridor, then looked down at his desk, leant forward with his elbows on the top of the desk and started crumpling a small sheet of paper.

Chapter Fourteen

DINO SPENT ALL AFTERNOON walking the streets of the city, without even going back to the site to change out of his work clothes. His feet followed one other calmly as they trod that sea of stones. In a way they never had before, the stones seemed to crunch like dry bones.

He walked beside the river for a long time, then along the ring road, and towards evening, as if everything was normal, he went to the billiard parlour, descended the stairs without taking his hands out of the pockets of his overalls, asked for the key, went to the table, took out the cue from its place, and sat down to wait for Cirillo so that he could lose his game.

"Is that how you're going around now?" Cirillo said, approaching the table, opening the display case and taking out his cue.

Dino gave a little laugh. "I left my clothes at the site."

Cirillo took a piece of chalk and gave the tip of the cue a

couple of strokes. "I see," he said. "You look a mess. I hope at least you washed your hands?"

Dino gave him one of his exasperated looks, although they were usually meant more as a joke than seriously. "Play, Cirillo," he said.

Cirillo looked at him. "What's the matter?" he asked, gravely, as he started arranging the balls for the game.

"Nothing, don't worry."

"If you like," Cirillo said, "I'll let you win."

"Fuck off, Cirillo. Play."

The game was like so many others—one perfect shot after another, with both men more interested in just being there, safe and secure, around that table and all its geometries, than in actually winning. But this evening, there was something else, a kind of distraction that moved from time to time between one ball and the next like a breeze, shifting the balls just a few centimetres from where they ought to have ended up.

Nearly halfway through the game, when Dino was ahead by a couple of points—not an unusual occurrence before the end—he stretched across the baize, ready to shoot, hoping he would hit two cushions and then Cirillo's ball. It was one of those awkward shots you made more in order to get into the cover than to score points, and which if you weren't careful might end up with your hitting the pins with your own ball and losing points to your opponent, but if you shot it well it made you feel really clever, for some reason.

The tip of the cue rested on Dino's bridge hand, just in front of the ball, and started to move backwards. Right at the bottom of Dino's index finger, just below the last bone, there was a small but deep bitumen stain he had not managed to get off even with soap. Without letting go of the cue, Dino lifted his hand slightly and scratched the skin where the stain was, hard, with his thumbnail, but without much success.

Cirillo frowned, wondering what the hell his friend was doing, trying to overlook the fact that he had never seen him break off just before a shot. "What are you doing?" he asked, standing on the other side of the table with his cue in front of him.

Dino's fingers froze. Then he ran his hand over the baize and put it together with his other hand at the edge of the table. He leant on the table, his arms as straight as posts, the cue propped between them, his head drooping. After a few seconds, he raised his head and looked at Cirillo. His eyes were those of a scared little boy. They didn't even seem like his eyes. "I can't do it, Cirì," he said.

Cirillo stood there on the other side of the table with both hands on his cue, not saying a word

"I can't do it. I can't spend every day in that black shit. It was different before. Before, everything seemed the way it ought to be. Before, I didn't ask myself any questions. Before, I spent the days counting how many stones it would take to make my child. Now I spend the days trying not to ask myself any questions, especially not how much more of that coal-black cancer I'll have to spread so that my child can have a life."

Dino let his head droop again between his arms, then flung the cue on the table and went and sat down on one of the chairs nearby. He threw his head back and took a deep breath.

Cirillo looked at Dino for another few seconds without moving, rubbing one lip against the other pensively, then propped his cue next to the scoreboard and went and stood in front of Dino, just a little away from him, with his bottom resting on the edge of the table and his arms and legs crossed.

Dino brought his head down and looked at Cirillo. It seemed to Cirillo that he was looking like a man again, maybe more like a man than ever.

"Listen," Cirillo said after a while, as if wondering if he should say what he had to say or not. "There's a tournament in a couple of weeks."

Dino frowned slightly. "A what?"

"A tournament," Cirillo said.

"A tournament? What kind of tournament?"

"A poker tournament. What kind do you think? A billiard tournament, you idiot."

Dino looked at Cirillo for a few more seconds, in an attempt to figure out was he was trying to tell him. "So what? We don't do tournaments."

"No, Dino," Cirillo said. "*I* don't do tournaments, you can do whatever you like."

Dino looked at Cirillo without saying anything, and swallowed a lump that had suddenly come into his throat and made him feel more alone than usual.

"It's called the Ingot Tournament, because the winner gets a gold ingot. They've been doing it every year for I don't know how long. You know how much a gold ingot is worth?"

"No," Dino said after a while, shaking his head.

"Quite a bit," Cirillo said.

Dino and Cirillo continued looking at each other for a while without saying anything, as if searching in each other's eyes for answers to questions they didn't even know they had asked.

"And what if I lose?" Dino asked after a while.

"If you lose," Cirillo said, "you carry on shovelling shit."

Chapter Fifteen

HE'D NEVER DO IT, Dino told himself. Inside that gigantic concrete edifice that was like the belly of a monster, three rows of shiny new billiard tables had been lined up, fifteen of them in each row. Above the rows of billiard tables were metal bars with large green lamps hanging from them, and the bars themselves were secured to steel tie beams which were up there somewhere in the darkness of the ceiling, amid immense ventilation ducts. The playing area with the rows of tables was cordoned off by high railings, and beyond the railings were concentric rows of terraced seating, the seats themselves funny little coloured things shaped like a person's backside. Even though there were hundreds of spectators, less than a fifth of the seats were occupied. This animal's belly seemed to come from a place that had little to do with this earth, and Dino wasn't even sure he would get out alive.

"Hey, you!" Dino heard from somewhere on his right, out of the din of voices echoing on all sides.

A tall thin man with grey hair and an electric-blue waiter's jacket was calling him.

"Yes?" Dino said, walking towards him with his cue in his hand, although of course, strictly speaking, it still wasn't his.

"Are you registered for the tournament?" the man asked.

"Yes," Dino said.

"Then go over there to that little table and give them your name. Quick now, it's late."

Over to the right of the lines of tables was a small table with a red cloth and some signs on it. Behind the table, two men were sitting, also wearing those funny electric-blue jackets, and in front were two long lines of people. Almost all of them were wearing shirts with coloured waistcoats and little ribbons, and all of them were carrying small cases.

Dino was still wearing the white shirt and brown velvet jacket that Sofia had made him put on for the occasion. He walked slowly between the rows of tables towards the two lines of people in front of the small table, looking around like a little boy and hoping that this vast animal's belly did not produce dangerous gastric juices.

He went to the end of one of the lines, leaning on his cue with every step, as if it were a mountaineer's stick. Two men from the other line looked him up and down as he took his place, then by chance their eyes met and they laughed and shrugged their shoulders. The one in front even seemed to shake his head. They, too, were wearing waistcoats and

rosettes. Dino wondered why they were all dressed like waiters, and felt rather out of place. He wondered if it was the
custom here, as if when you were in the belly of an animal
it was natural to dress like people bearing food.

"Card, please."

Dino had gradually moved forward until he was just in
front of the small table, and one of the men in the electric-blue jackets, a very short man the top of whose head
was as round and shiny as a billiard ball, which when you
thought about it was quite appropriate, was sitting there
with a large white exercise book full of columns and little
words, writing with one hand while holding the other out,
palm turned up.

"I'm sorry?" Dino said leaning forward slightly, still clutching his cue like a mountaineer his stick. A man in the other
line, who was also in front of the little table and was also
wearing a waistcoat and rosette, looked at him and smiled for
a moment, then went back to doing whatever he was doing.

The man with the round, shiny head slowly looked up at
Dino and was clearly surprised by what he saw. He looked
first at Dino's jacket, then at his cue without a case, and while
he was wondering where this character had sprung from he
said again, "The card. The licence from the federation. The
permit. The thing that says you can play."

For a moment, Dino felt like saying that he did not understand, then all at once it came back to him and he put his

117

hand in the large pocket of his jacket. "Oh, sorry, I forgot," he said with an embarrassed smile. "I only just got it."

"Of course," the man with the shiny head said, nodding. He took the card from Dino's hand and bent over to write again.

Dino glanced again at the other line and saw another man wearing a waistcoat and rosette take his card out of a small, elegant black leather case as smooth and soft as a baby's cheek, and once again he wondered what the hell he was doing in this place where everybody seemed to know a lot more than he did.

It had only taken Cirillo one day to get him the card. That was one of those things about Cirillo that Dino had learnt not to ask questions about over the years. A few years earlier, as he was waiting to lose his game, Dino remembered having a chat with another player at the bar in the billiard parlour. The man had told him that he was applying for a card to play in official tournaments, but that it was a long process, because among other things he didn't yet have enough games under his belt.

"Of course," Dino had said, although he hadn't the slightest idea what the man was talking about, and had completely forgotten about that chat later. It had come back to him, though, when, after only a day, Cirillo had handed him that damned card and wished him good luck in the tournament. Dino's first thought had been that it was better not to ask too many questions, then it had occurred to him that he didn't know how many games you needed under your belt to be worthy of that stupid card, but that he had surely played quite a lot of games, and so without giving it any more thought he had put the card in his pocket.

"Table twenty-three," the man with the shiny head said, giving Dino back his card. Dino took the card and thanked him, but barely moved.

"Over there," the man said, pointing behind Dino and to his left with his chin.

"Oh," Dino said smiling. "Thanks."

He turned in the direction indicated, with his cue in his hand.

Over every table, hanging from the metal bar next to the lamps, was a white sign with a number on it. Dino tried to find a logic in the sequence of numbers, but for some reason couldn't. He couldn't find a logic in the numbers, and he couldn't find a logic in all these people dressed like waiters, or in the dark sky filled with tubes in the belly of the animal, or in all the commotion that echoed in the air like the boom of a bass drum. Nothing here was like what he knew, and this rumbling stomach had no connection with that silent place where he played shots that were almost like prayers.

Dino stopped a couple of times as he walked past one or other of the tables and asked timidly if they knew where table twenty-three was. Each time, a man wearing a waistcoat and rosette looked him up and down with a puzzled stare, gave him a slow smile, and indicated a corner of the room. Dino thanked him, and both times, as he walked away, he heard the men behind him say something to each other and laugh. Dino felt the cold rise from inside his spine and bones, and apart from regretting that he had come to this hell filled with waiters, he also regretted that he hadn't brought a sweater.

"There it is," another man in a waistcoat and rosette said, pointing behind Dino with his chin.

Dino turned, and there before his very eyes was a splendid, brand-new table, which if it hadn't been for the green baize would have been as shiny as crystal.

"Thanks," Dino said, still feeling that sensation of cold.

At the end of the table, over towards the side where the terraces were, standing next to a large scoreboard, was another man in a waiter's jacket, although this one was white. "Card, please," he said.

"Of course," Dino said digging the piece of card out of his pocket.

On the other side of the table from the scoreboard, a man in a waistcoat and rosette was screwing together a strange faded yellow cue made from some weird material that Dino didn't recognise. Dino had often seen people come into the billiard parlour with these cues that were in two pieces, and when you talked to them they were ready to swear to you

120

that they were perfect and it didn't make any difference. Dino always nodded and said of course, even admiring in a way these objects which had to be assembled and which were in cases like violins, ready to play God alone knew what kind of music, but he always wondered how it was possible to get inside that dense forest of geometries as hard as oaks with a broken cue.

The man who was screwing together the cue had a funny round paunch and a huge black moustache that stuck out from the sides of his face like wings.

"Hello, Handlebar," another man in a waistcoat and rosette said, giving him a slap on the back on the way to the next table.

"Hi," the man with the moustache said, turning his head just a little and slightly raising his chin. He must be famous, a man with a reputation, maybe the kind of player who might even win the tournament, so well-known that everyone called him by his nickname. What had Dino been thinking? What had been going through his head? Did he really think he could play with professionals like these and hope to get anywhere? True, Cirillo was good, and in his way even famous, but you had to face up to the fact that even he had never played an official tournament. And even so, Dino had never beaten him.

As the man with the moustache turned back to his cue, his eyes fell on Dino, who was standing there staring at him.

121

The man looked him up and down, with a half-smile, then held out his hand.

"Hello," he said, almost chuckling, without even introducing himself.

"Hi," Dino said, shaking his hand with what little confidence he had left.

The man who had given Handlebar a slap on the back approached again from behind him, also screwing on his cue, and, looking Dino in the eyes with a sarcastic little smile, said, "Are you sure you haven't come to the wrong place, with that stick?" Then he laughed and walked back to his own table.

The man with the moustache also stifled a laugh and lowered his head again.

Dino looked down at his Arlecchino, which looked more beautiful to him than ever. A stick? This was an Arlecchino, every player's dream. It wasn't a cue, it was a sword, a king's sceptre, a magic halberd. For a moment, Dino had a strong desire to grab it from the end with both hands and hack his way through that forest of ungodly waiters and out of this repulsive, gastritic stomach.

"Here," the waiter in the white jacket said.

"Thanks," Dino said almost angrily, pocketing the card.

Then the man in the white jacket opened a cardboard box, inside which were three billiard balls, cleaner and shinier than any Dino had ever seen.

"If you want to do a few practice shots … " the man in the white jacket said, placing the balls on the table with a red cloth.

"Thanks," the man with the moustache said, placing the tip of his cue on one of the balls and tapping it slightly to get it into position.

Dino turned, propped his cue next to the scoreboard and started slowly taking off his jacket. He had no desire to see how the great Handlebar played. He would take off his jacket calmly, and very slowly start to roll up his shirtsleeves. If that wasn't enough, he would take a piece of chalk and rub it a little into the hollow between his thumb and his index finger, as he had always done ever since he had started playing, and would continue to prepare himself as best he could, listening to the clicking of the balls behind him without turning to look at them.

"I'm fine," Handlebar said after a while.

Dino finished tucking his shirt inside his trousers, and when he turned with his cue in his hand Handlebar was watching him from the other side of the table with that half-amused, half-curious expression people have when they watch a child trying to cope with something bigger than him.

"If you like, you can do a few practice shots before you start," the waiter in the white jacket on his left said.

Dino looked at him as if suddenly remembering he was there and trying for a moment to recollect what he had said, then he frowned and shook his head. "No thanks," he said.

He wasn't sure he grasped the point of practice shots. As if, after all the games he had played, three or four shots could make any difference!

The man in the white jacket gave a puzzled frown, and on the other side of the table Handlebar laughed a little and lowered his eyes.

"Are you sure?" the man in the white jacket asked.

"Pretty sure," Dino said.

The man frowned for a moment, then, almost imperceptibly, he raised his chin and held out his hand in the direction of the table. "Then get ready to start," he said, regaining his pride.

Dino nodded slightly, and went round to the other side of the table, again using his cue like a walking stick.

"White or yellow?" Handlebar asked Dino with affected politeness.

"Doesn't matter," Dino said.

Handlebar frowned, and the sides of his big moustache went down. "Then I'll take this one," he said, resting the tip of his cue on the white ball in front of him and moving it into position.

The break shot would decide who started the game, all you had to do was send the ball across the table to hit the opposite cushion and get it to come back as close as possible to your own cushion. The closest ball was judged the winner and opened the game.

Handlebar, like most players, put his ball more or less in the centre of his own half of the table, so that he got a good stretch across the table and was able to shoot as comfortably as possible. Dino, on the other hand, placed his ball very close to his own cushion, thinking this was a good opportunity to play one of those break shots he'd practised so much and bring the ball back to the same position from which it had started.

"All right?" the man in the white jacket asked, when Dino, too, looked ready to shoot.

"Yes," Dino said with a nod.

Handlebar turned his head towards him for a moment, nodded, threw a quick glance at the man in the white jacket, and then moved his eyes back to the ball, shaking his head a little as he did so.

"When you're ready," the man in the white jacket said.

Dino and Handlebar moved their cues backwards and forwards a couple of times, slowly, and then almost at the same moment hit their respective balls, which moved away as if of their own accord and started to travel towards the opposite cushion.

Dino straightened up a moment before Handlebar, then both stood watching to see which of the two balls would get closest to the cushion, with that unusually close attention common to gamblers.

The first ball to touch the opposite cushion, of course, was Handlebar's, which had had less distance to travel, but Dino's seemed to be chasing it as if eager to overtake it. By the time the two balls were nearing the end of the journey, almost at their own cushion again, they were almost level.

Handlebar's ball gradually slowed down and, as if someone had breathed on it, stopped just a couple of centimetres from the cushion. Dino's ball, on the other hand, still had a touch of inertia, and not only went past the point from which it had started but hit the cushion, rebounded off it and travelled another few centimetres before it finally stopped.

"White wins," the man in the white jacket said. "Ball to Giannini."

Dino looked at his own ball, a few centimetres from the cushion, but in relation to the position from which it had started actually about ten or twelve centimetres, and nodded to himself. He would have to be careful—the fresh cushions and the new baize, and perhaps even the different air in that gastritic stomach, made the ball go a bit faster than normal—not much, but just enough to shift the trajectories worryingly in a more complicated shot.

The man in the white jacket walked to their side of the table. "Will you take the white?" he asked Handlebar.

"Yes, thanks," Handlebar said.

The man in the white jacket picked up the ball in his red cloth, cleaned it, and put it back down on the table in front of Handlebar, then went to the yellow ball, cleaned that one, too, and put it in its place with a weird wooden stick with a hole in the middle.

"All right," the man in the white jacket said, when everything was ready. "You can start."

Handlebar tapped the ball, moving it until it was just in front of the middle of his own part of the table, more or less where he had started his break shot, but a lot closer to the castle. Then he stopped for a second, took what seemed a deep breath, stretched across the table and placed the cue on his bridge hand. Dino hadn't noticed it immediately, but Handlebar, like many of the players at the other tables, was wearing a strange small shiny glove which covered only three fingers, obviously to help the cue move more easily. It seemed to Dino that all these players took a lot of care over details, and once again he felt terribly out of place. Handlebar touched the cue to the ball, which set off determinedly towards the opposite cushion. It grazed Dino's ball, which moved to the left, and came back towards the bottom right-hand corner, but slightly too fast.

When both balls were still, Handlebar raised his eyes to Dino, who looked first at the table then at him. Handlebar walked to the end of the table with a barely concealed smile hovering over his lips, wondering what his opponent was going to do.

Dino stood there for another second without moving, wondering what Handlebar was smiling about, wondering above all if his leg was being pulled. The balls were both in cover, but both quite a distance from where they should have stopped. It was awful. Dino couldn't remember anything more awful. He had always been used to seeing almost perfect trajectories and lines on that damned green baize, cathedrals and classical sculptures with geometries so impeccable as to be quite moving. Seeing those balls so far from where they ought to have been was like hearing a pianist skip three chords in a sonata.

It must have been a deliberate tactic, Dino told himself, and for a moment he felt even more insecure than before. Cirillo had always described the great players as sly, untrustworthy people, ready at any moment to trick you, to stab you in the back and steal your wallet. That was how it had to be in this case—Handlebar must be putting on a mask to distract Dino and play the decisive shot at the most opportune moment. Dino would have paid any sum of money to be more ruthless, to have enough experience to see his way in these blind alleys and find a more effective method than the only one he could think of—to play as simply as he knew how, not think too much, and hope that everything went well.

Dino went close to his ball, stroked the tip of the cue a couple of times with the chalk, then bent and placed the cue on his bridge hand, just in front of the ball. It was a straightforward shot—across the table diagonally, hit two cushions then the opponent's ball—the kind of shot where it wasn't worth spending too much time sizing it up, because he had shot so many of them that he had the points of reference without even looking. Once, he had even tried to shoot one with his eyes closed, and all things considered it had gone quite well.

The sounds of clicking balls around him faded out, and as happened every time Dino leant over the table ready to shoot, he had the feeling he could hear notes coming from somewhere far away, as well as the deep murmur of his own breathing. A nice turn to the outside, a little push, and away it went. *Clack. Thump. Thump. Splat. Flop.* Eight points, as clean as music.

Handlebar's ball stopped just a few centimetres beyond the castle, just where it was supposed to be, like a mathematical theorem.

Handlebar was as still as a statue, staring at those fallen pins and that ball a few centimetres from the castle, then, after a few seconds, as the man in the jacket awarded points in a loud voice and walked to the table to stand the pins back up, he raised his eyes to Dino and stared at him.

"Ah," he said.

Chapter Sixteen

THE BILLIARD PARLOUR was completely empty and silent, and the only table that was still lit was the one occupied by Dino and Cirillo. Dino had promised his friend that whatever happened, and whatever time it was, he would drop by and tell him how things had gone, and if he did come in maybe lose a game, too. Now they were both in that island of light, both with their cues in their hands, at opposite corners of the table, Dino leaning on the edge and Cirillo smoking a small cigar he had been given by a plump gentleman he had been chatting to at the bar. They seemed like two old soldiers who hadn't seen each other for a long time, standing there telling each other stories with a smile on their lips and no desire to go to bed.

"It's incredible," Dino said, shaking his head a little, an amused look on his face.

With two fingers, Cirillo took the cigar out of his mouth and blew out a cloud of smoke, then gave a little laugh, looking at Dino without saying a word.

"They really don't have a clue," Dino said, still with the same amused expression.

Cirillo gave another little laugh, then took another puff at his cigar and blew out some more smoke. "I told you," he said.

Lying there motionless on the edge of the table, not far from Dino, was a shiny gold ingot, which seemed to cast more light than the big green lamps.

None of the seven people that Dino had had to play against to win the tournament had managed to gain more than fifteen of the fifty points they needed. A tall man, not very old but with prematurely white hair, had scored only three, and then only because, by an unexpected stroke of luck, his opponent's ball had decided to roll onto the red ball, otherwise he wouldn't even have scored that much. The only one who had managed to get fifteen points had been Handlebar.

By the time Dino had reached the quarter-finals, that small handful of journalists who were reluctantly covering the event were already going crazy, looking left, right and centre for information about this strange character who played in his shirtsleeves and with an old, brightly coloured wooden cue which was apparently called an Arlecchino, although none of them were old enough to remember it. Suddenly, that handful of journalists, all of whom would, up until then, rather have been anywhere else than slumped in their seats or dangling a microphone in front of some mediocre player and asking stupid questions, were brought back to life by this incongruous individual who cradled his cue as if it were made of crystal and mowed down his victims like a hero in a storybook.

By the time he reached the final, Dino was already on his way to becoming a legend. Already, like the great old players, as he approached that last table, the only one still lit, to face his last opponent, he had been greeted with cheers and applause from an admiring public. Apparently, some had even summoned their friends and relatives to come and see the prodigy, and one sick old player had even risen from his bed one last time to see the final, terrified perhaps at the thought that Dino might disappear back into the dark wood from which he had come.

The other finalist had been an impressive-looking character with a broad forehead that hung over his face like a sea wall, also dressed in a waistcoat and rosette and also with that strange three-fingered glove. He hadn't managed to score more than twelve points, and then only in the second of the three games they had played in the final.

When Dino had finished the last game, scoring ten easy points with a straightforward shot he had performed almost irritably, the whole audience in that gastric belly had risen to their feet and started applauding, whistling, and yelling "Bravo!" No sooner had the chairman said a few words and presented Dino with the ingot than Dino had been surrounded by journalists and photographers bombarding him with questions and blinding him with flashlights.

"Where are you from?"

"Where did you learn to play like that?"

"How did you learn to play like that?"

"Will you continue?"

"Why have you never entered any other tournaments?"

Dino had screwed up his eyes and sheltered them behind his hand, trying to find a way out of that frenzy and get a bit of peace and quiet.

"At home," he had replied. "Practising break shots. I don't know. Maybe. I don't know. I have to go. Excuse me ... The baby ... "

Somehow Dino had managed to escape from that quagmire, clutching his cue step by step until he found a way out.

When he was out on the street again and walking home alone, he had suddenly felt happy and at the same time dirty, and for some reason it was a sensation he would never again be able to free himself from. It was like discovering from one moment to the next that the perfection of numbers could cross the threshold of everyday life and bring a kind of order to things, and yet, as always, at the very moment when that perfection had entered the world, he had the feeling it had somehow made itself dirty.

"Yes, you told me," Dino said, nodding resignedly, as Cirillo, still smiling, took another puff on his cigar. "But I don't know if I really like it."

Cirillo nodded, too, then, as he put his cigar down on the edge of the table and was just about to stretch out again to shoot, he wondered once again if he had done the right thing, sending Dino into that slaughterhouse.

The next morning, after spending half-an-hour longer than usual in bed with Sofia, feeling the dome of her belly pressing on him and finding a whole new order and system of numbers and proportions in which to fit things, Dino got up and set off unhurriedly for the site. He waved to Carlo and Johnny from a distance, embraced Blondie, telling him he was really sorry, and then, very calmly, went to see Giani. He stood in the door of the office without even going in and looked Giani in the eyes. Giani put down the phone, saying that he would call back.

"I'm quitting," Dino said, still with one hand on the door.

"Dino, don't talk crap," Giani said, already looking down in the mouth.

"I'm not talking crap, I quit."

"But that's ridiculous," Giani said. "There's no need."

"Yes, there is a need," Dino said, giving him a last wave and closing the door behind him.

Chapter Seventeen

T HEY HEARD THE NEWS one day towards the middle of the afternoon, while Dino was helping Cirillo with the accounts. Dino was spending all day at the billiard parlour now, helping out, sorting a few things that had needed sorting for a while now. From time to time, he would go out with his Arlecchino—which still wasn't actually his—and win a tournament and make a bit of money. He'd bought Sofia some new clothes, and had even had her shop repainted. The dome of Sofia's belly was growing before their very eyes, and she carried it around with her as if it had always been there, with the same ease with which she cut material for a dress or a skirt.

Whenever Dino played a tournament, he would leave as silently as he had arrived, muttering a quick thank you if he had to and lowering his head when those damned cameras started flashing. But someone had found out where Dino played, and every now and again a journalist would show up and ask after him.

"He isn't here," they would always say at the bar or the entrance.

The journalist would look around. "That's not possible. They told me he's always here."

"He isn't here," the barman, Sandro, would say, shaking his head.

"What are you talking about?" the journalist would continue, looking around. "There he is. Over there."

He would make a move in that direction, and whoever was there would put a hand out to stop him.

"Maybe we haven't understood each other," the person would say, looking him straight in the eyes. "He isn't here."

Usually the journalist would give up almost immediately. Just once, Sandro and Mori had had to grab one of them, lift him bodily and march him up the stairs, while he went on about freedom of information and threatened to report them to the authorities.

That afternoon, though, everything had been quiet. Dino had sat at the bar counter, with a large exercise book and a few sheets of paper in front of him, trying to explain to Cirillo how to turn around the fortunes of the billiard parlour, although without making much headway. The idea had hovered there for a moment, only to be dismissed with a shrug of the shoulders, as if nothing was wrong, and everything had gone back to the way it was.

Dino never read the newspapers. Even after the ingot tournament it had been another customer of the billiard parlour who had brought in a whole lot of cuttings, saying that it had been thirty years since billiards had last featured on the front page, and giving Dino unexpectedly mixed feelings.

"They planted another bomb in the town hall," a man drinking a glass of soda at the bar suddenly said. He was a short, skinny man who moved like a salamander.

For a few seconds, Dino continued pointing to numbers in the big exercise book in front of him, then both he and Cirillo turned towards the skinny man with the soda.

"What are you talking about?" Cirillo asked, with a frown.

The skinny man put his glass down on the counter and stared at them for a moment. "There's been another explosion at the town hall," he said. "This time apparently it's bigger."

"Who says so?" Dino asked, his pen in mid-air over the numbers in the big exercise book.

"People," the skinny man said. "They also say they know who it was."

Cirillo and Dino looked at the man again.

"Who?" Cirillo asked.

"I don't know. Apparently, an old lady saw something."

Dino and Cirillo looked at the man, then exchanged glances and went back to the exercise book with the numbers.

"People never understand a damned thing," Dino said.

"Wise words," the skinny man said with a nod, taking a last sip from his soda. He threw a note down on the table and headed for the exit saying, "See you."

"See you," Cirillo said, and for a moment Dino watched the man walking to the stairs, then went back to the exercise book.

In the end, with a lot of patience, Dino managed to drill something into his friend's stubborn head. Later, as he was going back home after stopping at the butcher's to get two slices of meat for himself and Sofia, he told himself that life was a funny thing, but if you really thought about it and tried to find a logic in it, however obscure that logic was, you almost always found it.

But the funniest thing was that this new balance which Dino had seen taking shape in front of his eyes, and which was really quite solid, was only to last a few moments. For the rest of his life, Dino would have given any sum of money, would have given up part of himself, to go back to that moment, to stop on the pavement, perhaps with the key already in the door, and close his eyes and contemplate one last time that precise, orderly system, made up of perfect geometries which, out of the emptiness of sidereal space, had forged themselves a place in his universe of stones. He would have liked to turn back to that moment, if only for a second, to hear his own breathing and the beating of his heart and lose himself one last time, as if in the greatest of masterpieces, in that system of trajectories shining in space like rays of light. But for the rest of his life, he would see that damned key enter that system like a scythe cutting through those rays and those trajectories which were like threads of illuminated crystal, leaving only gleams of darkness as sharp as blades.

The door opened slowly. In front of him was the stone staircase that led to the first-floor landing. He did not even have time to put his foot on the first step.

"Boss," he heard a voice say behind him.

Peering into the dark corner next to the door, he saw the thin, narrow face of Blondie.

"Blondie," Dino said, "what are you doing here?"

"I need help," Blondie said, in that deep voice that seemed to belong to someone much older.

"What's wrong?" Dino asked, with a frown.

"What's wrong is, I have to go. Put bomb."

For a moment still, Dino stood there looking at that thin boy with the voice of a man, trying to grasp those two words that bounced around in his brain and sent a shiver down his spine. "What have you done?" he said, frowning again.

"I put bomb," Blondie said, without showing any emotion.

Dino looked at him in silence, hoping for a moment that this boy as hard as cast iron would disappear and the one he knew from work, who laughed as he splashed water on Duilio, would return.

"Are you crazy?" Dino asked, raising his voice. "What the hell do you mean, 'I put bomb'?"

"I keep eye, Dino, on your ... how you call him? ... councillor. He buy new car, find bigger house. Johnny right, Dino—black asphalt shit is kickback. Shit people in your town hall."

"And you think that's a good reason to plant a bomb?" Dino screamed.

"Speak quiet, please," Blondie said, with no change in his tone of voice.

Dino stared at him for a few seconds, then collapsed onto the second step of the stone stairs, put the meat he had bought for dinner down by his side, and put his elbows on his knees and his head in his hands.

"You help me?" Blondie asked.

Dino raised his eyes and stared at him for a moment. "Fuck off, Blondie," he said.

Blondie stared back at him. "If you not want to help, you say. I go away right now."

Dino was silent for a while, screwing up his eyes, perhaps unconsciously wondering if a crack had not already started to appear in the system. Then he looked at Blondie again.

"What do you want?" he asked.

Blondie stared at Dino for a moment without saying anything. "I need to escape. Old woman say she saw tall thin guy with long hair climbing gate of town hall."

"Is it true?" Dino asked, looking Blondie up and down.

"Don't know, but I tall, thin and with long hair."

Dino looked gravely at Blondie, wondering if he should laugh or punch him.

"They say police put roadblocks everywhere," Blondie said.

"Quite right, too," Dino said, giving a last glance at Blondie, then he looked down again and fell silent. For a moment, his eye fell on the bag with the meat, which he should have taken upstairs for dinner, and he thought of his wife and child upstairs calmly waiting for him to return.

Dino passed a hand over his face one last time, and when he opened his eyes again he looked back up at Blondie. "All right," he said getting to his feet. He took a bunch of keys from his pocket and walked to the other side of the banisters. "Come."

He went to the end of the little corridor between the wall of the entrance hall and the flight of stairs, turned left and opened a little door, painted white like the wall so that it was hard to see from a distance. He reached an arm inside and switched on a light. A little narrow stone staircase descended steeply between half-peeling walls.

"Wait down there, I'll see if I can think of something," Dino said without even looking Blondie in the eyes. Blondie stepped forward and started walking down, taking care not to bump his head.

"Oh," Dino said as he was about to leave. "This is the cellar of the building. At this hour, nobody should come down

143

here, but if somebody does come, do me a favour, make up some excuse, and don't do anything stupid."

"Don't worry," Blondie said, laughing. "I not kill."

"All right," Dino said, switching off the light and slamming the door.

Chapter Eighteen

S O DINO FOUND HIMSELF out on the street, in the evening, with a bag of meat in his hand and only one dumb idea in his head about what to do.

He walked across the centre of town as fast as he could, already feeling the sweat forming on his forehead, sure it would pour down him as soon as he stopped. He came to the big grey apartment blocks that filled the southern outskirts of the town, and stopped outside one of them. A group of boys passed on the other side of the street, and Dino wondered if he should feel worried, then for some reason, as he rang one of the bells, it occurred to him that the friend of a bomber had nothing to worry about, as if some of Blondie's gunpowder had started circulating in Dino's veins.

The entryphone beside the little iron gate crackled. "Yes?"

"Saeed, it's Dino. Come down here a minute, please, it's important."

There was a sharp noise from the entryphone, then silence, and after a minute or two Dino saw the dark figure of Saeed emerge out of the darkness of the stairs.

"Hi, boss," Saeed said when he was closer.

"Hi, Saeed. Something's happened, I need help."

Saeed gave Dino a worried look. "Sure, boss. Anything you want. What happen?"

"Did you hear about the explosion in the town hall today?"

"Yes, they say another bomb."

"Yes, Saeed. Blondie planted it."

Saeed's face grew, if possible, even longer than usual. "What the fuck you talking about?"

"Blondie planted the bomb. I'll explain later. Right now, though, the idiot's in my building. He says he has to get away, an old woman saw him and everyone's looking for him and he needs help."

Saeed looked Dino straight in the eyes. "Why you come to me?" he asked, gravely.

"Because apart from Duilio you're the only person who knows Blondie and who I could imagine would help me. But if you don't want to, Saeed, that's all right. I don't know if I want to either, but it's different for me."

Saeed and Dino looked at each other for a while, each man probably thinking about what he should do, trying to find some kind of common position without weighing it down with too many words. Saeed was wearing a tight white T-shirt that made his muscles bulge even more than usual and in the evening light made his face look even blacker.

"What you thinking?" Saeed asked, lowering his voice slightly.

Dino was motionless for a few more seconds, wondering if their silent conversation had led to something good. "I was thinking of the three-wheel van you use for the site."

Saeed nodded a couple of times. "What if they stop you?"

"If they stop me, tough. I'll tell them I had to work late on the site and that I'm going to unload the rubble now because I need the three-wheeler first thing tomorrow morning."

"Is total bullshit," Saeed said.

"Yes, Saeed, it's total bullshit. But what do they know? They're policemen, not bricklayers. Plus, I can't think of anything better. Can you?"

Saeed was motionless for a moment, looking at him as if suspending judgement, then shook his head.

"Is there any rubble on the site?" Dino asked.

"Yes," Saeed said in an almost thin voice, without taking his eyes off Dino.

"Good," Dino said.

Saeed stared at Dino some more, then turned his head aside and said something angry-sounding in his own language.

"Yes, I know," Dino said when Saeed turned to look at him again, even though he had no idea what he had said.

"Boss," Saeed said, "I take you to site. I open gate and fetch three-wheeler. But I not coming. I spend ten years here, trying to live regular life. I have family, and family not agree with bombs. I open gate and you go, and if something happen, you stole three-wheeler because your idea and because you know where I keep three-wheeler because you my friend. I tell my wife I never left home, all evening with her, she do this. Don't do something stupid. If they stop you and Blondie, is your business. Him terrorist and you thief who help terrorists."

Saeed and Dino looked each other in the eyes for another second, gravely, like two soldiers fighting a war that wasn't theirs.

"All right," Dino said, "that's only fair."

Saeed nodded and drew an unusually deep breath. "Wait here," he said, going back towards the big grey building and disappearing again into the darkness of the stairs.

Dino looked up at the sky and gazed at the few stars visible between the tall buildings and the thunderclouds. He would have given anything at that moment to be in front of a billiard table, right here in the middle of the street. Just to be able to take a few steps, grab his Arlecchino, lean across the baize and make a good shot, not too much force, starting from an angle, first cushion, *thump*, second cushion, *thump*, third cushion, *thump*, opponent's ball, *splat*, pins, *flop*, cover. To be back, if only for a moment, in that world where things went as they were supposed to and there were specific rules, a world where chaos and bad luck had no place.

After a few minutes, Saeed came back down, wearing a jacket. "Let's go," he said, with a nod of the head, without stopping.

They started walking fast, and their steps struck the stones of the street like horses' hooves. From time to time they passed someone, and each time Saeed sank down behind the collar of his jacket.

"You should have put your hat on," Dino said in a whisper as they passed the umpteenth person.

"White people not recognise black people in darkness. But everyone recognise black man with hat."

He had said it without turning a hair, Dino thought, and immediately wondered how it was possible that everyone always seemed to know more about things than he did. Every now and again, he had the feeling that whoever was responsible for the ingredients of life had given him only a third of what the other people had, or had forgotten to pass on some of the recipes, and actually this was something that bothered him quite a bit.

Fortunately, the place where Saeed was working turned out to be fairly close. A long, high wall of corrugated iron surrounded the site, an old farmhouse on the outskirts of town that was being renovated. Dino had always heard that it was an old ruin which had been sequestrated because of some terrible event that had taken place there and which was the source of a dispute involving lots of people. Apparently, the whole thing had now been cleared up and someone had bought the house, which was actually a fairly decent piece of property.

"Do you know anything about this house?" Dino asked as Saeed fiddled with the padlock of the big steel chain on the corrugated iron gate.

"What I supposed to know?" Saeed asked, glancing quickly at Dino.

"I don't know," Dino said. "I heard there was a big court case with a whole lot of people."

Saeed gave Dino another, almost irritable glance, then took the padlock off the chain and with a great clatter of metal ran the chain through one hole and left it dangling from the other.

"Boss," Saeed said, with a resigned, almost exasperated sigh, looking Dino right in the eyes and holding the gate half-open with one hand. "I hear someone in town hall buy this house. I hear many things, but I don't give shit, I forget, because I family and want to live peaceful."

"Ah," Dino said, as Saeed, a touch irritable now, finished opening the gate and disappeared inside. Again he had the unpleasant sensation that everyone knew more about everything than he did and once again that something was cracking, spilling acids that, in all probability, would gradually corrode whatever they met.

"Come," Dino heard Saeed say from inside the corrugated iron gate.

All the external plasterwork had been stripped from the house and was gradually being replaced by stone. Part of the roof still had to be done, and all around the house there were heaps of sand and rubble.

The big blue three-wheel van was parked to the right of the house, half hidden by the facade. Saeed went round to the side, opened the door, reached a hand inside and pulled on the gear stick.

"Come," he said again. "Give me a hand, we push three-wheeler to heap of rubbish, not to make mess."

Dino looked in the direction Saeed had pointed. Next to a shed, there was a little mountain of rubble and dust and earth that was waiting to be carried away. Dino nodded, walked to the three-wheeler and started pushing hard, while Saeed pulled from the door and every now and again gave a few turns to the steering wheel to move the three-wheeler where he wanted.

"Good," Saeed said when the bed of the van was close to the heap of debris. He again reached inside the three-wheeler and gave another pull on the gear stick. "Other shovel over there," he said, pointing to a corner of the shed, while he walked around to the rear of the three-wheeler and pulled a shovel from a hole just over the back transmission.

They began shovelling all the debris and earth that they could onto the bed of the van.

"How about also throwing in a bit of good earth?" Dino asked after a few minutes, more as an excuse to stop for a moment.

Using the same excuse, Saeed stopped and leant on his shovel. "Better not," he said after thinking about it for a moment, wiping his forehead with his sleeve and puffing a little. "If police stop you and policeman smart, he recognise good earth and get suspicious."

Dino looked at him gravely. "You're right," he said and went back to shovelling rubble onto the bed of the van.

When they had finished they both leant on their shovels, breathing heavily and wiping their faces with whatever they had. Then for some reason they smiled at each other, and then shook their heads and even laughed a bit, their laughter echoing in the silence of the evening as if they were in the theatre.

"Do you have a plastic sheet?" Dino asked after a while, still with a half-smile hovering over his lips.

Still panting, Saeed frowned. "Maybe yes," he said, and put the shovel down on the bed of the three-wheeler and disappeared inside the house. By the time he came back, carrying a big sheet of transparent plastic folded several times into a perfect square, Dino had grabbed a trowel from somewhere and for some reason was knocking a hollow brick into shape.

"Here," Saeed said, coming level.

Dino raised his eyes towards Said. "Thanks, just throw it inside," he said, then bent and gave the brick another knock with the trowel.

Saeed threw the plastic sheet into the bed of the three-wheeler, over the pile of earth, then looked at that funny, mixed-up little man he would always think of as his boss. He watched as Dino gave a last little knock to the brick, which was now practically half the size it had been before, examined it, got to his feet, carefully laid it down in the bed of the van, secured it with the plastic sheet, and rubbed his hands to wipe them clean.

"OK," he said, turning to look at Saeed. "I'm going now."

"Yes," Saeed said.

The two men looked at each other for a moment in silence, thinking with some part of themselves that they really belonged in another story, but that this one wasn't too bad after all.

"Thanks," Dino said, holding out his hand.

Saeed took it and gave it a firm shake. "You're welcome, boss. And be careful."

"Yes," Dino said. "Don't worry."

Dino opened the door and got in the front seat, which was actually more like a bench.

The three-wheeler started up, spluttering and juddering as always, in a way that aroused a certain sympathy.

"Maybe tomorrow morning I can bring the three-wheeler straight to where you live," Dino said with an amused little

153

smile, his elbow on the window and his other hand on the wheel. "That way, they won't see me come to the site."

"OK," Saeed said, smiling. "Drive safe."

Dino gave a little laugh, and Saeed gave two slaps on the bonnet of the three-wheeler, which resonated with the impact, then walked back to the gate and opened it.

"Goodnight, Saeed," Dino said as he drove past his friend, who was holding the gate open.

"Night, boss," Saeed said.

Chapter Nineteen

DINO DROVE BACK ACROSS the town centre, the three-wheeler backfiring in the darkness, and drew up in a little alley next to his building. He got out of the van, closed the door, walked round to the front of the building and put the key in the front door, looking around to make sure there was nobody nearby, and went inside. He went to the far end of the entrance hall and opened the cellar door, then reached an arm inside and switched on the light.

"Who is it?" a deep voice came from the bottom of the stairs.

"Father Christmas," Dino said, seeing Blondie's head emerge from behind the corner, and actually felt like laughing. "Do you think it's a good idea, when you're supposed to be hiding, to ask who it is when someone comes in?"

Blondie grunted something and started coming up the stairs.

"How's it been?" Dino asked, when Blondie had climbed a few steps.

"Everything OK," Blondie said, throwing him a slight smile. "Only kill couple people, but clean everything."

This time, Dino could not hold back the laughter, but when the boy was almost at the top of the stairs, he grabbed him and pulled him up by the elbow. "Don't be an idiot," he said.

Blondie smiled and dipped his head below his shoulders, as if to shield himself from a blow.

"And be quiet," Dino whispered as he switched off the light and closed the cellar door.

"Wait," he said still whispering, as he approached the front door. "I'm going to make sure no one's about." He pulled back the catch and slowly put his head out and looked right and left, then right and left again but more slowly. Then he raised his hand, inside the building, as if to say stop, and was silent for a few seconds, listening. There was nothing to be heard in the air but the nocturnal respiration of the town, that silent rumbling like the monotonous breathing of an old man.

"It's OK," Dino whispered. "Let's go."

They both slipped out through the door, as if wriggling out of a box, and, hugging the wall of the building, reached the alley where the three-wheeler was parked.

"Here," Dino said.

Blondie gave him a puzzled look.

"Let's just make a little space in the middle," Dino went on, moving the brick and the plastic sheet to one side. Then he leant over inside the back of the three-wheeler, took out the shovel from the pipe over the transmission and holding it at shoulder-height started to hollow out a valley in the middle of the debris.

Blondie watched him, still puzzled, without saying a word, wondering once again like thousands of others if this strange person, his boss, was a genius or completely stupid, or even crazy.

"Stand over there and don't move," Dino said after a while, continuing to excavate his valley.

When there was a trench running the whole length of the bed between two parallel piles of debris, Dino turned towards Blondie and wiped away a drop of sweat trickling down his temple. "Come," he said. "Lie down here in the middle."

Blondie looked at him again, still puzzled.

"Hurry up!" Dino whispered more loudly. "We don't have all week."

Blondie moved away from the wall against which he had been leaning, walked to the side of the three-wheeler, climbed in, clambered over one of the two heaps of debris, and lay down in the middle like a dead man in his own coffin.

"You completely crazy," Blondie said, looking at Dino with a vaguely worried expression.

"I'm not the one planting bombs, you idiot," Dino said, putting the shovel aside and walking around the back of the van. He bent down to the ground, pulled up the plastic sheet, unwrapped it, and laid it over the bed. Then he got in the back, put the brick to one side, and started to tuck the sheet around Blondie, who lay there as still as a corpse, still with that worried look on his face. When Dino reached Blondie's head, he pulled the sheet up a bit, sized it up, then grabbed it with both hands at the level of Blondie's mouth. He took a penknife from his pocket—he always carried it with him—and, taking care not to slice through his finger, cut the sheet just below where he was holding it, making a small hole. Then he smoothed the sheet out again and tucked it under Blondie's head. The little round hole rested just over Blondie's mouth.

"Can you breathe?" Dino asked, looking Blondie in the eyes through the semi-transparent sheet.

Blondie nodded without saying a word. He looked more like a corpse than ever, and for a moment Dino hoped it wasn't any kind of omen.

Dino turned and grabbed the brick, moved it close to Blondie's head and told him to take it. Blondie gave him another puzzled look and did not move.

"Take it!" Dino whispered again, loudly, waving the brick in front of Blondie's eyes. Blondie moved his hands slowly from his sides, as if trying to push his way out from under a barber's gown, and grabbed the brick.

"Congratulations," Dino said, letting go of it. "Now put it over your mouth."

Blondie did not move.

"Hurry up," Dino whispered again. "Rest one of the holes over your mouth."

Blondie again moved his hands slowly and placed the brick on his face. From inside the brick he could be heard sighing softly.

"Can you breathe?" Dino asked, quickly tilting his body first to one side, then the other, to make sure that his invention was working as it was supposed to.

Blondie nodded, looking Dino in the eyes through the sheet, said a soft "Yes" through the hole in the brick and gave a little laugh.

Dino smiled, pleased with his invention. "Now keep still and don't move for any reason until I uncover you. Have a nice trip." He patted Blondie's side twice and jumped down from the van.

"Bye," Blondie said from inside the brick, with another little laugh.

Dino picked up the shovel and, looking around to make sure nobody was about, completely covered Blondie in a single heap of earth and debris, from the top of which the half-broken brick peeped out for a few centimetres, although nobody would ever notice it, expect Saeed.

When he had finished, Dino stuck the shovel back in the pipe at the back of the three-wheeler, then gave a last tap to the brick and said into it, "We're leaving. Don't worry."

He got in the driver's seat and started the engine and, with a lot of grumbling and backfiring, the three-wheeler began reversing out of the alleyway. He passed the door of his building, rumbled through the side streets and slowly headed westwards, driving alongside the river for a while. It seemed a particularly quiet evening, and seagulls were circling between the bridges.

Chapter Twenty

I T WAS SOME TIME NOW since the rumble of the three-wheeler had stopped echoing between the walls of the houses and had been swallowed up by the wider spaces between the warehouses on the outskirts of town. Dino felt almost relaxed now, thinking that perhaps he had been over-zealous, and that no one was going to search for a bomber, to search for anyone for that matter, if they didn't even know what the person looked like. So he opened the window and put his elbow out to feel the coolness of the night on his face and was looking forward to a brief excursion into the country, when from the end of the street, just where one of the last warehouses gave way to the first cultivated field, he saw the outlines of two police cars.

A uniformed officer walked quickly into the middle of the road and ordered the three-wheeler to stop. Dino's heart started pounding in his chest, and that pleasant coolness he had felt just a moment earlier suddenly became an icy current that howled through his nerves and veins.

"Hello there," the officer said. "Switch off the engine, please." He was quite a tall, thin man, with hollow eyes and a thick grey moustache.

"Of course," Dino said, bending slightly and groping for the key, knocking his hand on the wheel as he did so.

"Can I see your papers, please?" the officer said when the three-wheeler had finally shuddered into silence.

"Of course," Dino said, putting a hand in his pocket.

The papers. How was it possible he hadn't thought of that? How was it possible he hadn't thought of the one thing you needed if you ran into the police? For a moment, as he leant to his right, praying that the papers were where they ought to be, he remembered that moment of amused self-satisfaction when he had seen how the brick and the sheet worked out. Now he wouldn't find the papers, which were the only things that mattered, and he would start to stammer some embarrassed excuse and they would become suspicious—another policeman, shorter and stockier than the first one, was already walking towards the back of the three-wheeler—and they would ask him to get out ... and there the documents were, in the little drawer in front of the passenger seat, all dusty and creased, but shining with a light that no sheet of paper had ever had.

"Here," Dino said, with a clear sensation of heat on his skin, like a tropical breeze. He took a deep breath. "Nice weather we're having."

The policeman took the papers, thanking him. Then all at once he frowned and looked Dino straight in the eyes. "Yes," he said, nodding slowly. "Nice weather."

The policeman looked at Dino for another moment from the corner of his eye then walked off towards the cars to check the papers and confer with his colleagues.

In the rear-view mirror, Dino saw the other policeman looking in the bed of the van and almost distractedly moving a few bits of rubble with his truncheon.

The tall policeman with the moustache came back, and the two of them approached the window.

"Where are you going at this hour?" the policeman with the moustache asked, handing Dino the papers back, while the other one stood a little further back, looking at him gravely, with both hands on his truncheon.

Where was he going? How should Dino know where he was going?

"I'm going to unload some rubble at the dump."

"Now?"

"We were working late, the councillor wants the villa ready the day before yesterday, so we even have to work at night." Dino didn't know where that thing about the day before yesterday had come from, but all things considered he liked it, and for a moment he even thought of swearing and spitting on the ground, but then changed his mind.

"Aren't there any dumps in town?" the policeman further back said, in a harsh, sibilant voice that seemed to belong in a different story altogether.

"At this hour? If you know of one open, then tell me, because I can do without having to drive around in the middle of the night, damn it," and this time he did spit on the ground, hoping he wasn't exaggerating. "A few kilometres from here," he went on, pointing down the road, "there's a dump that's always open." Dino knew his story wouldn't stand up, but he hoped the policemen didn't know too much about the subject.

"All right," the policeman said. "You can go. Have a good evening."

"Good evening my arse," Dino said. He had started to get a taste for this. "Thanks anyway." He started up the three-wheeler, and the two policemen nodded gravely and watched him drive away.

Dino even put his hand out of the window to wave goodbye, and as he pulled it back inside, with even the last warehouse now behind him, along with a smile and another warm breeze Dino seemed to see a meadow strewn with daisies growing on the rumbling bonnet of the three-wheeler. Life wasn't so bad really, and maybe you never knew where a new theorem capable for a moment of putting things in order might emerge from. You expected theorems to emerge from places and dynamics with precise co-ordinates, instead of which for some reason they might spring up even from a noisy clapped-out old three-wheeler.

Chapter Twenty-One

Dino had been chugging along for several kilometres now in the middle of the countryside, past tilled fields and occasional patches of scrub, when all at once, along a white side road, in a clearing half covered with a clump of poplars, he stopped the three-wheeler and listened to it spluttering in the night as it fell asleep.

The door squeaked as he opened it. He walked to the back of the three-wheeler, took the shovel from the pipe just over the transmission, rolled up the sleeves of his jacket and started throwing the earth and debris and rubble to the sides of the bed. Before long, Blondie's legs, then his trunk, still under the dusty sheet, saw the light of the countryside. Finally, Dino put the shovel to one side and with his hands freed and dusted off the part of the sheet covering Blondie's face, then took off the brick, put it to one side and, grabbing the top of the sheet from behind Blondie's head, pulled it away, uncovering the whole body.

"Go on, son," Dino said. "You're free."

Blondie lay there for a moment looking at Dino, then sat up, still staring at him. "You genius," Blondie said.

"Forget that," Dino said. "Get out of that thing, I need to empty it." He started folding the plastic sheet as best he could.

Almost in a single bound, Blondie stood up and jumped out of the three-wheeler like a cat, then picked up the shovel, unhooked the back flap, and started unloading the rubble and earth.

"Are you doing that?" Dino asked as he finished folding the sheet.

"Yes," Blondie said, and for a moment they both felt the way they used to when they had worked together on the roads, placing stones in the wet earth.

When he had finished, Blondie put the shovel back in the pipe and went up to Dino, who was leaning calmly and silently against one side of the three-wheeler, looking up at the sky.

"Thanks, boss," Blondie said, also leaning back against the side of the van, breathing hard.

"Forget it," Dino said, then lowered his eyes and looked at the boy. "Listen, I'm sorry to drop you here. I'd have liked to drive you all the way to the border, but with this contraption it would have taken too long."

"Is OK, boss. You do too much. You real friend."

Dino nodded, then again raised his head and looked up

at the sky. "It's a nice night," he said.

Blondie also looked up. "Yes," he said, "is nice night."

For a while they stood there motionless, staring up at the stars. From the fields around them they heard the sound of crickets. Every now and again, an owl hooted.

"You have cigarette?" Blondie asked.

"No," Dino said. "I'm sorry."

"You not smoke," Blondie said. "Is good."

Yes, maybe it was good. And yet at that moment, standing there sweaty and dusty, with this whole mess behind them and an uncertain future ahead, a cigarette wouldn't have gone amiss.

"I don't know," Dino said.

They looked at the sky a while longer, then Dino lowered his head and glanced at Blondie. The owl hooted again.

"Listen," Dino said. "Tell me something."

"Yes," Blondie said.

"Where the fuck did you find a bomb?"

Blondie also lowered his head and after looking down at the ground for a moment or two threw a glance at Dino. "I build," he said.

"I what?"

"I build."

"What do you mean, *I build?*"

Blondie threw another glance at Dino. "I mean, I make bombs with jars and liquids and spare parts we find around.

169

Little bombs."

"Oh," Dino, said staring for a moment at Blondie's thin profile.

"I bomb expert."

"I what?"

"Bomb expert. You deaf."

"Fuck off," Dino said smiling.

Blondie also smiled.

"What do you mean, you're a bomb expert? Where?"

"At home."

"In the army?" Dino asked, glancing at Blondie.

"Revolutionary army."

"Oh," Dino said, and for a few seconds stared down at the stones and earth in front of his feet. "Why did you come here?" he asked after a while.

"I was prisoner," Blondie said. "Managed to escape, but tired of war, and when outside told my comrades I leaving."

"And what did they say?"

"They understand. They tired too."

Blondie and Dino exchanged a quick glance, then Dino nodded and looked up again at the sky. "And now?" he asked after a while.

· "Now I go home."

"Oh," Dino said, then turned for just a moment to Blondie.

"Same shit everywhere," Blondie said after a while, picking up two or three stones and throwing one into the fields. "If

170

my job putting bombs, better I put bombs in my country," he went on, throwing another stone and watching it land in the field in front of him, then turned towards Dino.

"Doesn't turn a hair," Dino said, staring for a moment at Blondie.

"Is better I go," Blondie said. All at once he seemed older and taller, and when Dino moved away from the side of the three-wheeler to embrace him, it seemed to him that he was hugging an old friend.

"Please," Dino said. "Don't fuck things up."

Blondie squeezed Dino and gave a laugh. "Of course I fuck things up," Blondie said. "Is our fate fuck things up."

The two men separated and Dino gave a little laugh. "OK," he said. "Then be careful you don't fuck things up too much."

Blondie smiled and looked at Dino for the last time. "Yes, I be careful," he said, and he put his hands in the pockets of his jacket and started walking along the white road.

"Bye, Blondie," Dino said.

Blondie turned and for two or three steps walked backwards, without stopping. "Bye, boss," he said.

Dino watched him walk away, then after glancing up at the sky again and at the countryside all around, he opened the door, which squeaked again, and got back behind the wheel.

Chapter Twenty-Two

I T FELT GOOD, driving around in the three-wheeler. It would be nice to fill it with luggage and go off with Sofia to all those places they had dreamt of going. They could even take the baby with them. Dino could build a metal framework with clamps that could be welded to the bed of the van, he thought as he passed the police cars and happily raised his arm and waved to them, and Sofia would be able to sew a rainproof sheet to put over it.

By the time he was again gliding between the tower blocks, with the river just visible in the distance, Dino was convinced it would be great, and he saw himself charging around the world with his family in the three-wheeler. Sofia might even be able to hang a few flowerpots somewhere.

As he drove alongside the river, glancing at the seagulls with his head slightly out of the window, it struck Dino that it was an absolutely perfect picture, a precise, sharp-edged equation like the strictest rules of mathematics, perfect, immutable proportions, resisting any slight—three people within the triangle of a blue three-wheel van.

Dino climbed the stairs of his building with that fleeting sensation of being someone who, at least for a moment, has seen how things really are, and has sensed despite himself, in a fold of the world, a rule that puts together all the pieces of the mosaic. As he looked for the key to his apartment door, he decided he would tell Sofia straight away. She must be in bed, worried probably that she had not seen him or heard from him all evening, but as soon as she heard him get into bed and he told her about the three-wheeler she would certainly start laughing, and as always after a while would come up with some brilliant idea to add to the programme. They would probably start fantasising, drawing roads on Sofia's swollen belly, using it as a globe. Maybe after a while she would even get out one of the travel books and make a few notes, Dino thought as he unlocked the door of the apartment, trying to make as little noise as possible. Then, while they were talking about the three-wheeler and where they would go, they might even make love. But Sofia wasn't in bed, Sofia was lying face down on the floor of the living room, between the sofa and the little wooden table. It was an image that took a few seconds to reach its destination, as if after all those fantasies the world had to take the time to fall back into place. Dino stood motionless and bewildered in the entrance for a few seconds, with one hand still on the door. A large blotch of dark liquid surrounded Sofia's belly and legs, impregnating her clothes, and a sickly metallic odour seemed to be everywhere.

All at once the world finished falling back into place, and the image of Sofia lying face down and motionless in a pool of dark, sickly liquid hit Dino's stomach like a battering ram.

Dino thrust his chest out and gave a cough that had come from somewhere deep in his guts. He slammed the door behind him and ran to his wife.

"Hey," he said, bending down next to her, but there was no answer.

He turned her over. Her face was pale, and her hollow eyes stared at him as if they were open.

"Oh," Dino said, kneeling there, supporting her head with one hand and stroking her cheeks with the other. He bent over her mouth and her chest, trying to hear if she was still breathing and if her heart was beating.

"Shit," he said, resting her head back on the floor.

He stood up, ran into the bedroom, lifted both blankets off the sheet with a single gesture and went back into the living room. He laid the blankets over his wife, slipped an arm under her legs and one under her shoulder and got to his feet. He reached the door, opened it, turning his hand under Sofia's body, walked out onto the landing, kicked the door shut with one foot and descended the stairs. He repeated the operation for the front door of the building, crossed the street and laid his wife on the bed of the three-wheeler. He tucked the blanket in on either side, in such a way as to protect her from bumps, then opened the door, took the plastic sheet from the passenger seat, folded it firmly one more time, lifted Sofia's head a little and laid it on the sheet.

"It's all right darling," he said. "Don't do anything stupid."

He got back in the three-wheeler, put in the key and, as soon as he felt the engine leap into life, set off as quickly as he could. Every few seconds he glanced back through the glass window behind him, and observed his wife lying like a corpse on the bed of the three-wheeler, struggling in silence against something he could only guess at.

From time to time, the three-wheeler hit a pothole that was a bit deeper than the others, and Sofia's body was jolted more than it should be.

"Sorry, darling," Dino would say out loud at the window behind him. "We're nearly there, don't worry."

He should have been there. He shouldn't have been driving around saving his bomb-making revolutionary friends, he should have been at home saving his wife and child. He shouldn't have allowed any variation. Precise, simple rules. The shortest route possible for the best result. Two cushions, ball, pins down, in the cover. A simple shot. Cover, always in cover. There is no gain without cover. Simple precise rules. No bombs. No rushes of blood to the head. Carefully calculated shots, then cover. Bad luck doesn't exist. If you make a mistake it means you played a bad shot.

When the three-wheeler pulled up in front of the door to the emergency department, two males nurses dressed in white were standing outside, smoking and chatting.

"Hey!" they cried, almost running out of the way for fear the three-wheeler would run them over.

"Come on, darling, come on," Dino said, breathlessly, as he got out of the three-wheeler and lifted his wife out of the bed of the van. "Come on," he said again in her ear as he walked away from the three-wheeler with Sofia in his arms.

"What happened?" one of the male nurses asked, throwing away his cigarette and coming towards Dino.

Dino kicked the door wide open and rushed inside like a bandit.

"I need a doctor!" he screamed once he was inside. A handful of weary-looking people jerked their heads up to look at him.

"Don't worry, we're here," one of the male nurses said, while the other went to fetch a trolley. "What happened?"

Dino turned, dazed, to look at the nurse. He had a round, soft face and a fatherly expression.

"I found her like this," Dino said.

The other nurse approached with a trolley. "Put her down here," he said.

"What happened?" the round-faced nurse said.

"I don't know," Dino said. "I came back home and she was in a pool of this dark stuff."

"What month is she?" the other nurse asked, starting to push the stretcher towards a large double door of opaque glass.

"The seventh," Dino said.

"And what happened?" the round-faced nurse asked, pushing a large red button to open the opaque glass door.

"I don't know," Dino said. "I was out."

"All right, don't worry. You just sit there. As soon as we know anything, we'll tell you," the round-faced nurse said, and he disappeared through the opaque glass door, swallowed up by that oesophagus full of people in white and green coats rushing back and forth.

"I was out," Dino said again in a thin voice, watching the opaque glass door close.

After a few seconds he lowered his eyes and put his hands in the pockets of his jacket, and before turning to sit down listened to the sound of his own breathing and the loud beating of his heart.

The people in the waiting room wall had all been looking at him, but when he turned to find a seat they looked away. Dino walked back across the room, settled in an empty seat in the far corner and sat with his hands in his pockets, looking down at the floor.

A thin white-haired old lady, who might have been even older than the lines on her face indicated, leant slightly towards him, lightly touched his leg and smiled. "Don't worry," she said in a sharp but quite clear voice. "Everything will work out in the end, you'll see."

Dino looked up for a moment and smiled, then looked down at the floor again.

Chapter Twenty-Three

T IME PASSED. After more than an hour, the old lady's husband came out. He had a cloth cap on his head and a big plaster on his right arm. The old lady patted Dino on the leg and said, "Cheer up," then went to her husband and walked him out of the hospital.

A few people were discharged and a few others arrived, among them two parents carrying a little boy in their arms. The boy was in pyjamas and had a bandage on his head.

"He fell out of bed," they said to the people around them as they sat down, with those intense, polite smiles typical of parents.

"Hello," Dino heard someone say to him at last. It must be nearly dawn by now, and Dino had his elbows resting on his knees, with his head dropped forward. Two black leather shoes had appeared in front of him. Dino slowly raised his head and found himself looking at a tall, grey-haired man in a white coat.

"You're Sofia's husband, aren't you?"

The doctor was looking at him with an expression that Dino could not decipher. He had his hands in the pockets of his white coat, with the thumbs outside.

"Yes, I am," Dino said.

The doctor gave a slight smile and held his hand out. "I thought so. Sofia's told me a lot about you. I'm the doctor who's been treating your wife. It's lucky I was on duty tonight."

"Hello," Dino said as he stood up and shook the doctor's hand. "Dino."

"Yes, I know," the doctor said. "Come, follow me."

The doctor crossed the waiting room like an army general, also pressed the big red button and led Dino into that teeming oesophagus, which was a bit quieter now than before. He did not take Dino along the corridor, but turned left and pressed another button, a smaller black one, next to what appeared a metal door, and started to wait, first giving Dino a little smile, then looking down at the ground. After a few seconds, the metal door opened onto a small square cubicle which could not have been more than two metres by two metres. The doctor went in, waited for Dino to do the same, then pressed another button with a number on it. The cubicle gave a little jolt, and after a few seconds the door opened on to a corridor identical to the previous one, only emptier and more silent.

The doctor started walking along the corridor. They came to a half-open door, and the doctor put his hand on the handle and looked Dino straight in the eyes.

"I'm going to be quite frank with you," he said, his smile completely gone now. "Sofia is very ill. She had a bad haemorrhage, and lost a lot of blood. The machines are keeping her alive for now, but I can't tell you what's going to happen."

Dino felt a scythe suddenly plant itself in his side, and for a moment he felt as if the whole left side of his body had gone hard. "All right," he said, nodding and swallowing he didn't know quite what, in a voice that was not completely his.

The doctor nodded, too, and after a couple of seconds opened the door. The room was completely white, with an empty bed on one side and his wife's bed on the other. He seemed to be entering another dimension, in some fantastic future time, a time when machines lived lives of their own and stood by next to the beds of the humans, holding them by the hand with their tubes and their cables.

"Jesus," Dino said, slowly entering the room. A funny machine with a screen emitted strange pulses every now and again and a tube emerged from Sofia's slightly twisted mouth, fixed to her lips with white tape. The tube was attached to a little bag and every few seconds the bag would inflate then deflate quickly. The tube ended in another strange machine, with a kind of accordion inside it which rose and fell suddenly in the syncopated rhythm of the bag. There was another, smaller tube going from Sofia's arm to a little bottle hanging from a kind of coat rack, and on her finger there was a kind of clothes peg, linked to the wire from another machine. God alone know where all these machines were trying to take her, Dino thought.

Dino also thought that Sofia seemed quite peaceful, and that she was not the kind of person to be as relaxed as that with people she didn't know. That meant she must feel comfortable with those machines. He even thought of waking her up and asking her what she thought about it, then he told himself that it was better if she rested, and anyway, with that tube in her mouth, talking couldn't be much fun.

Dino looked at the white sheet neatly spread over Sofia's body and saw that, beneath it, that globe that he had stroked and listened to until the previous evening had suddenly disappeared.

"What about the baby?" Dino asked in a thin voice, feeling his skin turn to dry, cracked plaster.

"She's fine," the doctor said, just behind him.

Dino turned his head quickly towards the doctor, as if he had suddenly woken up. "Is it a girl?" he asked.

"Yes, it's a girl," the doctor said.

From somewhere, Dino found the strength to smile, then turned back to Sofia.

CHAPTER TWENTY-THREE

"Do you want to see her?" the doctor asked.

"Of course," Dino said, nodding, then went up to Sofia, told her he would be right back and walked to the door.

The doctor again led him to the little sliding metal door, pressed the button again, waited for the door to open, entered the square cubicle with Dino, pressed another button with a higher number and, when the door opened again, walked out into another corridor similar to the previous one. A nurse came out of a room with a bundle in her hand, and for a second Dino wondered if it could be his daughter, but the nurse went through another door while the doctor carried straight on. Through a large window at the end of the corridor, you could already see the red light of dawn starting to colour the distant hills and the silent walls of the town.

"Here we are," the doctor said halfway along the corridor.

Dino gave him a puzzled look, then realised that they were standing beside a large window, behind which was a dimly lit room full of gadgets and shelves and machines. In the centre of the room were two large rectangular transparent boxes, with canvas rings on the sides. Inside the boxes, if you looked closely, you could see the outlines of two tiny purple creatures, one in each box, which seemed too weak even to be held in one hand.

"She's that one there," the doctor said, pointing to the box on the right.

"Oh," Dino said, nodding and staring at that little wrinkled animal he would be calling his daughter for the rest of his life.

"You found her lying on her stomach, didn't you?" the doctor asked, watching Dino as he took a step towards the window.

"Yes," Dino said, tearing himself away from those mesmerising folds on his daughter's body and looking at the doctor. "How do you know that?

"From the position of the baby," the doctor said, then let a few seconds pass while Dino turned back, spellbound, to his daughter. "Your wife's body heat kept her alive. If she had been lying with her belly up, I don't know how things would have turned out."

Dino, still looking at his daughter, gave a slight laugh. "Typical," he said.

For another moment or two, the doctor watched this strange man with his hands in the pockets of his jacket looking at his daughter in the incubator. "What do you think?" the doctor asked after a while.

Dino was silent for a few seconds. "She's full of wrinkles," he said.

The doctor, too, gave a slight laugh, then both he and Dino stood for a few minutes in silence, looking at the dimly lit room in front of them.

"It might be a good idea to get a bit of rest," the doctor said after a while, leaning forward a little to see Dino from a better angle.

Dino did not move, his eyes still fixed on that transparent box and that little animal full of wrinkles. "Yes," he said after a while, taking a little step back. "It might be."

Dino and the doctor went back along the corridor to the sliding metal door, and the doctor again pressed the button.

"Can I see Sofia again for a moment?" Dino asked, throwing a quick glance at the doctor.

"Of course," the doctor said. "Go right ahead."

They went back to Sofia's room. There she was, as still as before, surrounded by the same machines.

Dino went to the side of his wife's bed, leant down towards her head and whispered something in her ear that the doctor could not hear. He moved a hand over her forehead, gave her a kiss, then turned, put his hands in his pocket and started for the door.

"Thank you," he said as he passed the doctor and walked through the door. "Everything's fine."

For a moment, the doctor wondered what exactly was fine. But then it struck him that this was no time to be asking himself so many questions.

When they were back downstairs, across from the main entrance, Dino turned to the doctor and held out his hand. "Thank you," he said again, with a sudden pride. "You're a good person."

The doctor almost felt like laughing, but managed to restrain himself, more or less. "You, too," he said, giving Dino's hand a firm shake.

Dino looked him straight in the eyes. "I don't know about that," he said, and the doctor couldn't think of anything better to do than give a weak smile and watch Dino as he disappeared through the door.

As soon as Dino was outside, he realised that when he had arrived he had left the three-wheeler right there, and now it wasn't there. Luckily he only had to take a few steps to see it parked in a decent spot a few dozen metres away. A good Samaritan must have moved it while he was somewhere inside. Maybe it had been the male nurse.

When he reached the three-wheeler, he saw that even the blankets he had carried Sofia in had been put back in the driver's compartment. Unfortunately, they still had that sickly smell that had come from somewhere in her belly.

As he was looking at the blankets, Dino noticed a crumpled, dust-covered white bag under the passenger seat. It took him a few seconds to recognise. He reached down and picked up the bag and placed it on his lap. For a moment he looked at it the way we look at an archaeological find, or rather, the way we look at an object which belonged to us as children, and which we find again dozens of years later—with the same mixture of curiosity and emotion. Dino slowly unfolded the bag, until he had opened it completely, and laid it down as best he could on his thighs. Inside, there were two big slices of red meat, just a little wrinkled by the folds of the paper. Dino sat looking for a few seconds at that red, bloody meat, then actually passed a finger over it and pressed down. It was strange, it was as if he didn't recognise these slices, as if they came from another place entirely and had somehow crossed the border. After a few seconds he lifted the whole package and even sniffed it. It didn't smell of meat, it smelled of some bizarre synthetic material, maybe—if you dug into the matter—with a clear hint of metal.

Dino dropped the open bag and the meat on the passenger seat, next to the blankets. Then he started the three-wheeler, reversed out of his parking space, with the usual spluttering noises, and as he left the hospital car park picked up the bag with the meat and threw it behind a bush.

It was quite late by now, and Saeed must have been at the site for a while, Dino thought. In fact when he arrived Saeed was already there waiting for him. Fortunately, nobody else had arrived yet.

"How did it go?" Saeed asked when Dino got out of the three-wheeler with the blankets in his hand.

"Fine," Dino said, almost without looking at him. "Thanks."

"And those?" Saeed asked, indicating with his chin the dirty blankets Dino had in his arms.

"Nothing, forget it," Dino said, already moving away with his back to the site. "Thanks, Saeed."

Saeed watched him walk away with regular, precise steps, staring straight ahead, and for some reason he preferred not to ask himself any questions.

Chapter Twenty-Four

WHEN DINO GOT HOME, he went straight to the
bathroom, threw the blankets in the bathtub, filled
it with warm water and emptied a handful of soap powder
into it.

Then he came back to the living room, flung the window
wide open, went to the kitchen to get a rag and a bucket,
came back to the living room again, shifted the sofa and
bent down to clean up that pool of dark, sickly stuff that
covered the floor.

In the end, he had to take the rug from under the low
table in the living room and throw that in the bathtub, too.
He spent all morning cleaning and tidying the apartment,
even dusting the shelves and behind the jars in the kitchen.
The apartment had not been so clean and tidy for years, in
fact Dino couldn't remember when. Once the blankets and
the rug had been wrung out and hung outside to dry, Dino
undressed and had a bath.

Then he got dressed with the first things he found in the wardrobe, closed all the windows in the apartment and set off for the billiard parlour.

He gave Sandro a hand in arranging a couple of things in the bar, looked through the accounts for a while and spent much of the afternoon tidying a box room where bundles of papers and various other objects had accumulated over the years. He also found a dusty old cup with a figure of a man leaning to shoot a ball and a plate with the words *First Prize*. Cirillo came in while Dino was sitting on one of the big boxes, holding the cup and dusting it off as best he could with his hand.

"Hey," Cirillo said after a few seconds, leaning against the doorpost with his shoulder.

"Hi," Dino said, looking up at him for a moment, then down at the cup again. "What's this?"

Cirillo frowned a moment. "What?" he asked.

"This," Dino asked, holding up the cup. "You said you never played in a tournament."

He said it with an almost sarcastic smile, as if he had caught his friend with his hand somewhere it shouldn't be.

Cirillo turned the cup over in his hands, then put it to one side and threw it a last look. "Dunno," he said, then looked back at Dino, who had stood up and gone back to work.

"And you?" Cirillo asked.

"Me what?" Dino said.

"How are you?"

Dino bent down to pick up a large box. He hoisted it onto his knees and put it on one side, raising a new cloud of dust. "Everything's fine, Cirì. Don't worry."

"Sure?" Cirillo asked, peering at him from the door.

"Sure," Dino said.

Cirillo watched him for a while longer, then, thinking it was none of his business anyway, turned to go.

Dino carried on tidying the room for the rest of the afternoon, then when he was tired and had stacked most of the papers again, he decided to call it a day.

He left the room, switched out the light, went to the bar, picked up his jacket from the stool where he had left it, calmly put it on, waved to Sandro and made to leave.

"No game?" he heard Cirillo ask behind him.

Dino stopped for a moment, turned his head just a little, then carried on up the stairs. "No," he said.

Chapter Twenty-Five

D INO WALKED BACK across town, trying to look around as little as possible and to think as little as possible about the stones he was stepping on.

He got to the hospital sooner than he had expected. As he had the night before, he went in through the main entrance, walked to the opaque glass door, pressed the big red button as if he was at home, and once inside headed for the sliding metal door.

"Excuse me," a voice called to his left, while Dino was waiting for the metal door to open. "Where are you going?"

A nurse was quickly coming towards Dino, frowning.

"To see my wife," Dino said, looking the nurse straight in the eyes.

"Oh," the nurse said, suddenly slowing down, her face tightening as if she had just been slapped. "Go ahead," she said, almost in a whisper, while the doors of the lift opened, unable to take her eyes off Dino.

"Thank you," Dino said, disappearing behind the sliding metal door. Once inside, Dino pressed the button with the number he had seen the doctor press those few hours earlier, and for a moment wondered if there was some connection between that number and this whole business.

When the sliding metal door opened again, Dino got out and walked down the corridor to the door of Sofia's room.

Everything was unusually silent. You could even hear the evening breeze rustling the leaves of the trees outside.

Sofia was still motionless and peaceful in her bed, but the machines weren't there any more. Even they had gone away. Maybe she had been the one to send them away. Maybe she had wanted to be on her own for a while. Maybe she had wanted to be silent for a while. That was quite characteristic of her. Dino had often seen her walking by herself along the river. And God alone knew how many times he'd come back home and found her leaning out of the window in the living room, the one that looked out on the roofs of the town and the hills in the distance. Once, Sofia had told him that she could spend hours on end at that window. Dino had often wondered what she saw in those roofs and those hills. Then he had told himself that perhaps she saw what he saw in stones, or perhaps something else.

Dino took a few steps towards the bed. The sheet was covering Sofia up to the throat. It looked as if it was carved in marble. Only the features of his wife's face remained. God alone knew where she was. God alone knew if she was there watching him, as so many people said, or if she had flown away somewhere else.

"I'm sorry," Dino heard someone say behind him, and the words fell into the emptiness, like the coins he used to into the well in the centre of town when he was a young boy. He heard them clinking dozens of metres down, then that silence returned that had more the smell of nothingness.

Dino did not say a word. He stood there, motionless, looking at the statue that someone had carved using his wife's face. The same cheekbones, the same drawn lips, the same scar over her left eye which she had got while playing as a little girl and which Dino liked so much. The same mole on the left temple and the same little lines that were starting to form next to her eyes and on her forehead. Even that funny hint of a smile she had on her face when she slept, as if every time she closed her eyes she went off to a more peaceful place. Maybe she was there now. Only the colour wasn't really hers, in the same way that, in Dino's opinion anyway, paintings, however beautiful, never managed to completely capture the true, vivid colour of skin, as if there was a strange iridescent mixture in skin that was impossible to reproduce. This almost greenish grey, with just a few touches of pink still left, had little to do with the soft glow of Sofia's skin. Dino had once told his wife that her skin was a highly unusual colour.

197

"There must be a place where they have the colours to reproduce it," Dino had said. "Maybe in India."

Lying back on her pillow, Sofia had looked at him and given a little laugh. "Yes," she had said. "Maybe."

Then while they were making love they had told each other that when they went to India they would look for colours to reproduce her skin.

But they had never been to India. They had never been to India or the North Pole or black Africa or beyond that to the end of the world. They had never been anywhere, and now she had got fed up waiting and had gone away by herself, leaving behind her that macabre statue with the same vague smile. Dino should have known she would go away sooner or later, he should have realised that all that talk about travelling would get to her sooner or later. What was there to stay for? To see the world crumble and the roads swallowed up by the Devil's slime and bombs explode and people with waistcoats and rosettes who didn't know how to play billiards? No, Sofia had done the right thing, or rather, she had done the only sensible thing—she had gone away, without thinking twice. She had waited for Dino for more than ten years, what else could she do?

Dino stood there beside his wife's body for a little while longer, trying to catch in that emptiness something that wasn't his own breathing, something that had the slightest taste of life. Then he took a step closer to the bed and moved his finger, first over Sofia's forehead, then over the clear lines of her nose and lips. He felt something well up inside him, and before everything exploded Dino closed every exit he knew. He took a long deep slow breath, then slowly let the breath out of his mouth and raised his head and looked straight in front of him like a soldier, out of the window and towards the hills.

"It's OK," he said, turning abruptly.

The doctor was there, looking at him with a vaguely worried air. "She didn't suffer," he said, trying to give a little smile.

"I didn't think so," Dino said.

The two of them looked each other in the eyes for a moment and the doctor nodded slightly.

"I'd like to see my daughter," Dino said.

"Of course," the doctor said.

Dino started walking quickly, preceding the doctor out of the door and towards the lift. They went up to the maternity ward and again walked as far as the window behind which his daughter was resting. She was still there, nice and peaceful, with all her wrinkles.

"I'd like to go in," Dino said.

"That's not possible," the doctor said.

"I don't give a damn," Dino said.

The doctor looked for a moment at the man standing there in front of him. Well, he thought, he may have a point. "Come on, then," he said. "We can go in through here."

He walked to a thick door to the left of the window and opened it. The door led into a room with a desk and various cabinets filled with bandages and instruments and medicines, and from that room another door led into the little room where Dino's daughter was.

"Go ahead," the doctor said, opening the door for Dino.

"Thank you," Dino said.

He entered the dimly lit room, and for the first time saw his daughter from close up. He thought she was the most incredible thing he had ever seen, and in the middle of all those wrinkles it seemed to him that he recognised Sofia's lips and smile. He leant towards the glass box and whispered something, then gave his daughter a last glance, turned and left the room.

"I'm going," he said when he was again in the corridor with the doctor. "I may be back in a while."

"All right," the doctor said, shaking Dino's hand. He watched him start to walk down the corridor. "Oh," he said after a few seconds, "there's still the matter of the name."

Dino stopped and turned to look at the doctor. He had already put his hands back in the pockets of his jacket. "The name?" he said.

"The name of the baby. We need a name for the birth certificate."

Dino looked at the doctor for a moment. "Names are a big con," he said.

The doctor gave a slight laugh. "Yes," he said, "maybe they are."

Dino nodded, then for a few seconds looked the doctor straight in the eyes, but as if he was looking at him from a long distance, still half-turned away with his hands in the pockets of his jacket. "Call her Grecia," he said after a while.

"Grecia?" the doctor said, with a slight frown.

"Yes, Grecia," Dino said.

"Why Grecia?"

"Don't worry yourself about it," Dino said, then turned and resumed walking towards the small metal door at the end of the corridor.

The doctor watched him disappear inside the lift, and wondered where he would go, if he would return to that parallel universe he always seemed to emerge from.

Chapter Twenty-Six

T HE STEPS of a distinguished-looking man echoed in
the silence of the night like the harsh ringing of a bell.

At the umpteenth stroke, Dino's eyes suddenly opened
wide. For a few seconds, he managed to move just his eyes—
up to the gutter, over the stones of the walls, the windows and
shutters of the building opposite, the pigeons sleeping on the
windowsills and the closed shop shutter and the newspaper
kiosk he was propped against. Searching silently for the
coordinates that would tell him where he was.

Once outside the hospital, Dino's legs had started to move
automatically and regularly, wandering the town with his only
concern being not to smash into the walls. Dino's hands had
never left the pockets of his jacket, and his eyes had remained
fixed on a spot a couple of steps in front of him.

The stones and the earth and the dirt and the street and
the pavements went past under his feet like a winter river,
with all their voices and their calls which Dino had no desire

to listen to. Dino had laid over his skin a layer of granite, while inside all his muscles and nerves were twisted and drawn and stretched and painful, in an attempt to stop the fire from spreading and blowing everything up, into millions of ragged fragments and sparks of bloody meat.

By the time he had reached the river he had become convinced that his poor army would lose the battle, and he already felt the heat of the fire burning his skin and getting ever closer to the powder keg, so close that for a moment he had been seized by the almost irresistible impulse to climb the little wall beside the river and drown the fire down there in the current.

He had barely found the energy to walk down two or three side streets, far from the river, before his body and the layer of granite that he had laid over it fell like plaster from a wall. He had leant with one hand on a lamp post, had felt every single muscle in his body crumple, the sides of his mouth drawn down, his eyes so taut they were almost bleeding, and as he felt his strength leave him he had just had time to fall in a sheltered corner of the pavement, thinking that, all things considered, it wasn't a bad way to die.

He had been given barely a moment to feel himself fall, and yet in that moment he had found time to say goodbye to the world, to see his body explode there in the middle of the street in a pool of blood and flesh, already weeping for the daughter he had not managed to bring up.

And yet now he seemed still to be alive, alive with the life that most human beings live. He moved his head away from the shutter behind him and for a few seconds looked around him again, trying to figure out if it was just an impression of his or if everything really was completely silent inside him. This really did seem to be his town, and he really did seem to be alive. Obviously he had only fainted, or something like that. He straightened his back and pulled his legs, which lay abandoned like rags on the pavement, towards him. He put his arms on his bent knees and listened to the air passing like music in and out of his lungs. There was still that black sense of emptiness that seemed to be trying to suck him in, but the fire appeared to be extinguished and the powder keg for the moment to be safe. Maybe his army needed forces he wasn't even aware of, and to obtain them he hadn't found anything better to do than put it to sleep. Maybe. But it wasn't really worth thinking about. Now he felt more tired than anything else, and when you came down to it, a life didn't seem so much more restful than a war.

He rubbed his face with his hands and took a deep breath, then opened his eyes again and looked at the building in front of him. He looked at it for a few seconds, then let his eyes fall to where he was sitting, looking for something. He stretched out his right hand, picked up a few pieces of rubble that had fallen off the wall a little further on, then, rolling slightly with his bottom and putting one hand on the ground, he got laboriously to his feet. He took another deep breath, and as he relaxed his legs he let his head fall first on one side then on the other, listening to his neck stretch and crack. Then he took a few steps into the middle of the road, looked at the front of the building, broke a piece of rubble and threw it against one of the shutters, hitting it slightly.

"Rosa!" he cried in a thin voice.

He looked around to make sure that nobody was coming, then took a larger piece of rubble, pulled his hand back and threw it with some force at the front of the building. This time he had caught the shutter full on and the piece of rubble exploded loudly in a cloud of dust.

"Rosa!" Dino cried again in a thin voice. After a moment, the shutter on the second floor opened slightly.

"Who is it?" a sharp voice came from behind the shutter.

"Rosa, it's Dino," Dino said.

"Idiot, it's four in the morning," the voice said. "Stop drinking and go to bed."

The shutters slammed shut.

"No, Rosa, stop!" Dino called, still in a thin voice, trying to summon up his strength.

The shutters opened again just a little.

"Who's there?" the voice said, as if it was made of stone.

"Rosa, I need a grandmother," Dino said, still in a thin voice, but yelling less.

"Piss off, Dino," the voice said, and the shutters slammed shut again.

"No, Rosa," Dino said, starting to yell again, then, slightly lowering his voice, "Sofia's dead."

It was the first time he had said it, and for some reason it had never seemed as true as it did now.

The shutters remained closed and still for a few seconds, then very slowly they opened completely, showing first two thin arms pushing them, then just above the windowsill Rosa's sharp, lined face in the middle of that halo of white hair.

"Dino, you shouldn't joke about things like that," Rosa said from behind the windowsill, although she already sounded a little anxious, less convinced of her rightness.

"I got home last night," Dino said, "and found her lying in a pool of dark stuff."

"What about the baby?" Rosa asked.

"The baby's fine. She was born early so they put her in a glass box to keep her warm."

"It's a girl?"

"Yes, it's a girl."

Rosa nodded from behind the windowsill and for a moment looked Dino straight in the eyes. "I'm coming," she said, then disappeared, pulling the shutters behind her.

Dino stood there in the middle of the road. He dropped the last pieces of rubble he was holding, beat his hands together a few times to get the dust off, then rubbed them on his legs.

After a few seconds he saw the shutter of Rosa's shop rising, making an almighty racket in the night, and beneath it there appeared first the slippers, then Rosa's thin legs, then her gnarled hand and her bowed head.

"Come in," Rosa said, motioning to him with her hand, before disappearing inside.

Dino walked to the half-raised shutter and bent down to get under it.

No sooner was he inside than he was overcome by that orchestra of smells that always played in Rosa's shop. After so many hours, he was pleased to hear something familiar.

Rosa was bustling about over a few vases. She picked out a dozen red and blue flowers and green leaves and heaped them up on the counter. Then she took some string and tied everything as best she could. She leant over to one side, got out a little bottle full of liquid the colour of which Dino found hard to figure out, placed it on the counter, walked to the last vase, took a little yellow flower, went back to the counter, pulled three petals off the flower, opened the bottle, and pushed the petals into it. Then she closed the bottle and placed it next to the bunch of flowers she had tied earlier.

"So," Rosa said with her hands on the bunch and the bottle. "Take this home and put it in a new vase. It'll do you good, you'll see. And this," she said, raising the bottle slightly, "put it close to the baby if you can, it'll help her. What have you called her?"

Dino looked at Rosa, wondering how she would take it. "Grecia," he said.

Rosa gave him a puzzled look. "Oh," she said. "All right, now, do you understand what to do?"

"Yes," Dino said.

He took two steps forward and took hold of the bunch of flowers and the bottle. "I don't know anything about children, Rosa," he said looking at her with vaguely frightened eyes.

"Don't worry, Dino, they know it all. There were a lot of things I didn't know, and I'm still here."

Dino gave a little nod, then tried to smile to thank her, said goodbye, and turned, taking with him the bunch of flowers and the bottle.

After a few steps, he stopped and turned again to Rosa, who was clearing the dead leaves off the counter. "Rosa," he said.

"Yes?" Rosa said, stopping what she was doing and half turning to look at him.

"Do you still have the three-wheeler you used to use for delivering flowers to people's houses?"

"Yes, the building manager has it in his garage."

"Would you sell it to me?"

Rosa frowned and looked at him for a moment. "If you're prepared to take it off my hands, I'll give it to you."

"All right," Dino said. "We'll talk about it again. Bye, Rosa."

"Bye, Dino," Rosa said, and went back to doing what she was doing.

Chapter Twenty-Seven

ONCE HE GOT HOME, Dino took a vase from above one of the cabinets in the kitchen, half-filled it with water, cut the string with a knife, and put the bunch of flowers in the vase. Then he put the vase and the little bottle, which he was still holding, on the table in the living room, and after moving the flowers around a bit it struck him, for the first time in that very long day, that he was hungry.

He went in the kitchen, sliced half an onion, and put it to heat in a frying pan with a little oil, then took three eggs, broke them in a bowl, and started beating them. As soon as they were ready, he poured them into the frying pan with the onion and watched to make sure they cooked the way they were supposed to. That was how he had always seen Sofia make them, and he hoped it was as easy as it looked.

When the eggs were almost completely hard, he took the lid of a pot out of a cabinet, and used it to turn the eggs over in the pan. He thought they were going to break completely and it would be a disaster, instead of which everything went fine, and when, soon afterwards, he plunged a fork into the eggs and lifted it to his mouth, it struck him that, all in all, he would manage somehow.

He ate standing in front of the window where Sofia usually stood. It was in fact a lovely view, and maybe if he found out how to read it he might discover something in it. He felt a kind of throbbing in his ears for a moment, and as he ate his eggs he started walking around the apartment, lost in thought. He stopped for a moment by the shelf on which over the years they had arranged their travel books. They were all there, lined up like real books, and Dino took one out as if everything was normal, as we might take out a photograph album in a friend's house. It was funny, in all these years he had never reread them, in fact now that he thought about it he wasn't sure he had even pulled one out before. As he put a forkful of egg in his mouth, with the other hand he opened the book on a page at random, just to see where he and Sofia had been fantasising about visiting more than a dozen years earlier. He read a few sentences. It wasn't really like a note at all, it was as if she was talking about places they had really seen. Dino ate the last mouthful of his eggs, then put the plate down next to him and started reading again with more attention. He couldn't quite figure out where they were, but Sofia's round handwriting definitely seemed to be describing the two of them in an inn, and a fat host who told them funny jokes in a language they only half understood. Other customers of the inn were also described, as well as Dino's expressions as he laughed at the host's jokes. Dino frowned a little, then skipped a few pages and resumed reading. Now, Sofia was talking about being very tired, and that missing that train had been a great bother. But that was the great thing about travelling, she said—you were constantly coming up against situations that you weren't entirely in control of. Dino and Sofia had never missed a train, nor had they ever planned to miss one while travelling, nor had they ever made comments and considerations about what travelling ought to be like, seeing as how they had never travelled. Dino looked up and examined the page from more of a distance, then looked at the row of books that had been put there over the years, which suddenly seemed like an encyclopaedia of something that Dino had never managed to grasp.

Dino took out the first of the books. He remembered very well the first journey they had started to dream up stories about, a journey to those countries in the north where the dawn seemed to last all day.

"We could go north," Dino had said.

"Yes," Sofia had said after a while, "we could go and see those places where they say the dawn never ends."

"We could," Dino had said more softly.

Instead of which, the notebook began like this: "At last we made up our minds to set off." And for some reason it struck Dino that it wasn't a bad idea to begin with an *at last*. But there weren't any *we coulds*. Instead, there were lots of details, lots of descriptions, as if Dino and Sofia had really been to those places. First, there were the descriptions of the preparations and the long journeys to get to those places, descriptions of the places where they had slept and eaten, even at one point a description a foreign couple with whom they had travelled for two days talking to each other only with gestures. It was quite funny, and a couple of times Dino caught himself laughing.

It was only after two or three hours, and quite a few pages, did Dino reach the moment when he and Sofia had finally seen those dawns that never ended, and for a moment, trying desperately to hold back the tears, it seemed to him that the sun would never again set, never again rise, but stay trapped forever in the limbo of dawn.

By now, he was sitting on the sofa with the notebook open on his knees. He closed it and for a moment sat there listening to his own sighing and looking at the black cover which contained secrets that he had never been able to solve.

He stood up and went to the window and as he stood looking out at the sun starting to illumine the roofs of the houses, he knew what he had to do. He took a deep breath, moved his neck again until it cracked, put on his jacket, picked up

Rosa's little bottle and the book and left home. It struck him that he was tired, but that this wasn't the moment to rest.

He went back to the hospital, pressed the big red button, went up to his daughter's floor, went in through the door next to the window and was about to go straight into the room where the incubator was.

"Excuse me," a nurse said as he was going in. "Stop."

As if what he was doing was quite normal, Dino took a chair from one side of the room and moved it close to the glass box where his daughter lay, nice and quiet, surrounded by her wrinkles.

"You can't stay here," the nurse said from the door of the room.

Dino looked her straight in the eyes. "Go and call security if you want," he said. "I'm not moving from here." He took Rosa's little bottle from his pocket, put it down on the floor, took the top off, and as the nurse went out muttering something he opened the book and started reading.

This was what he would do. As Sofia had decided to go away without revealing part of herself to him, he would force her to give him a hand in bringing up the baby. Suddenly the emptiness felt like less of a weight.

Chapter Twenty-Eight

T OWARDS EVENING, it struck Dino that now he was really tired and that the hour had come to rest, and he blew his daughter a kiss and left the hospital.

He started walking as if everything was normal, and once he got close to the centre of town, instead of going home, he turned in the direction of the town hall.

The big old building stood out in the air of the evening like a fat, squat man. To the right of the big dark wooden main door, next to what must once have been a big earthenware jar, there was a circular mark, as if it had been struck by a fist, and above this mark was a big black stripe that went up as far as the broken windows on the first floor. It was as if a big ball of heated stones had come from somewhere, and what remained was a strange burn mark that would be hard to erase. There was something sinister and fascinating about that circle of damaged wall and that vertical black brushstroke and those broken windows, as if there was something hidden in every loose piece of stone that drew you like a magnet.

Dino stood looking at that wound. He would have preferred it if it didn't have anything to do with him, and yet for some reason he felt proud to be a part of it. Maybe, all things considered, everybody likes to have the illusion that they belong to something great, something absolute.

After a few minutes, though, it struck him that maybe this was how things were—they were destroyed, and it didn't matter very much how, and above all there wasn't much that anybody could do about it. Then it struck him that before going home he wanted to drop into the billiard parlour for a moment, and he set off again as if everything was normal.

He walked in with barely a greeting for anyone, walked up to the table at the far end of the room, took his cue from the display case, took off his jacket, rolled up his sleeves, took the little tray with the balls, put it down on the baize, picked up the chalk, gave a few strokes to the tip of the cue, moved one of the balls closer to him, and after a moment's concentration, getting a clear idea of the ball's position, stretched across the table and put the tip of the cue on his bridge hand. He let the cue move backwards and forwards a couple of times, then released it. *Clack.* The ball set off calmly towards the opposite cushion, rebounded off it and gradually slowed down as it came back, until it had ended up in what seemed to be the exact same point from which it had started. Dino looked carefully at the ball sitting there, where he had always thought it ought to be. He leant forward and took a closer look at it, first from one side, then from the other. He straightened up and looked at the ball again. Then he went around the corner of the table and crouched next to the long cushion, carefully observing the ball from that angle and slightly tilting his head to one side. After a few seconds he straightened up again and, still looking fixedly at the ball, gave a few more strokes with the chalk to the tip of the cue, and again stretched out across the baize. The ball set off again, as before, towards the opposite cushion, hit it again in the same place and gradually came back and settled in what seemed to be the exact same place as before.

Dino looked at the ball again, and an almost imperceptible smile crinkled the corners of his eyes. He again turned the corner of the table and again crouched at the edge. He again tilted his head slightly to one side, and kept it in that position for few seconds, observing the smooth surface of the ball lying on the green baize. He could almost distinguish the single microscopic filaments that formed the material of the baize, and if he had been even more patient he might even have identified who had been the last person to touch the ball. For a moment, the lines of the material seemed like dunes in the desert, and as he looked at them in the shadow of the huge ball he shook his head and let out a little laugh.

"What's up, son?"

Dino looked up and saw Cirillo standing there beyond the table with his hands in his pockets. He looked up at him for a few seconds, still crouching there at the edge of the table. Cirillo tried to read the expression in Dino's blackened and hollow eyes.

"Why didn't you ever tell me?" Dino asked.

Cirillo frowned slightly. "Why didn't I ever tell you what?" he replied.

"That the ball never comes back to the same place," Dino said.

Cirillo let his eyes fall for a moment on the white ball in front of Dino, sitting there, nice and quiet, on the green baize, where it ought to be. Then he looked at Dino again and he felt the impulse to smile.

"You got so close, I didn't like to tell you," he said.

PUSHKIN PRESS

Pushkin Press was founded in 1997, and publishes novels, essays, memoirs, children's books—everything from timeless classics to the urgent and contemporary.

Our books represent exciting, high-quality writing from around the world: we publish some of the twentieth century's most widely acclaimed, brilliant authors such as Stefan Zweig, Marcel Aymé, Teffi, Antal Szerb, Gaito Gazdanov and Yasushi Inoue, as well as compelling and award-winning contemporary writers, including Andrés Neuman, Edith Pearlman, Eka Kurniawan and Ayelet Gundar-Goshen.

Pushkin Press publishes the world's best stories, to be read and read again. Here are just some of the titles from our long and varied list. To discover more, visit www.pushkinpress.com.

———

THE SPECTRE OF ALEXANDER WOLF
GAITO GAZDANOV
'A mesmerising work of literature' Antony Beevor

SUMMER BEFORE THE DARK
VOLKER WEIDERMANN
'For such a slim book to convey with such poignancy the extinction of a generation of "Great Europeans" is a triumph' *Sunday Telegraph*

MESSAGES FROM A LOST WORLD
STEFAN ZWEIG
'At a time of monetary crisis and political disorder... Zweig's celebration of the brotherhood of peoples reminds us that there is another way' *The Nation*

BINOCULAR VISION
EDITH PEARLMAN
'A genius of the short story' Mark Lawson, *Guardian*

IN THE BEGINNING WAS THE SEA
TOMÁS GONZÁLEZ

'Smoothly intriguing narrative, with its touches of sinister, Patricia Highsmith-like menace' *Irish Times*

BEWARE OF PITY
STEFAN ZWEIG

'Zweig's fictional masterpiece' *Guardian*

THE ENCOUNTER
PETRU POPESCU

'A book that suggests new ways of looking at the world and our place within it' *Sunday Telegraph*

WAKE UP, SIR!
JONATHAN AMES

'The novel is extremely funny but it is also sad and poignant, and almost incredibly clever' *Guardian*

THE WORLD OF YESTERDAY
STEFAN ZWEIG

'*The World of Yesterday* is one of the greatest memoirs of the twentieth century, as perfect in its evocation of the world Zweig loved, as it is in its portrayal of how that world was destroyed' David Hare

WAKING LIONS
AYELET GUNDAR-GOSHEN

'A literary thriller that is used as a vehicle to explore big moral issues. I loved everything about it' *Daily Mail*

BONITA AVENUE
PETER BUWALDA

'One wild ride: a swirling helix of a family saga… a new writer as toe-curling as early Roth, as roomy as Franzen and as caustic as Houellebecq' *Sunday Telegraph*

JOURNEY BY MOONLIGHT
ANTAL SZERB

'Just divine… makes you imagine the author has had private access to your own soul' Nicholas Lezard, *Guardian*

BEFORE THE FEAST
SAŠA STANIŠIĆ

'Exceptional... cleverly done, and so mesmerising from
the off... thought-provoking and energetic' *Big Issue*

A SIMPLE STORY
LEILA GUERRIERO

'An epic of noble proportions... [Guerriero] is a mistress
of the telling phrase or the revealing detail' *Spectator*

FORTUNES OF FRANCE
ROBERT MERLE

1   The Brethren
2   City of Wisdom and Blood
3   Heretic Dawn

'Swashbuckling historical fiction' *Guardian*

TRAVELLER OF THE CENTURY
ANDRÉS NEUMAN

'A beautiful, accomplished novel: as ambitious as it is generous,
as moving as it is smart' Juan Gabriel Vásquez, *Guardian*

ONE NIGHT, MARKOVITCH
AYELET GUNDAR-GOSHEN

'Wry, ironically tinged and poignant... this is a fable
for the twenty-first century' *Sunday Telegraph*

KARATE CHOP & MINNA NEEDS REHEARSAL SPACE
DORTHE NORS

'Unique in form and effect... Nors has found a novel
way of getting into the human heart' *Guardian*

RED LOVE: THE STORY OF AN EAST GERMAN
FAMILY
MAXIM LEO

'Beautiful and supremely touching... an unbearably poignant
description of a world that no longer exists' *Sunday Telegraph*

SONG FOR AN APPROACHING STORM
PETER FRÖBERG IDLING

'Beautifully evocative... a must-read novel' *Daily Mail*

THE RABBIT BACK LITERATURE SOCIETY
PASI ILMARI JÄÄSKELÄINEN

'Wonderfully knotty… a very grown-up fantasy masquerading as quirky fable. Unexpected, thrilling and absurd' *Sunday Telegraph*

STAMMERED SONGBOOK: A MOTHER'S BOOK OF HOURS
ERWIN MORTIER

'Mortier has a poet's eye for vibrant detail and prose to match… If this is a book of fragmentation, it is also a son's moving tribute' *Observer*

BARCELONA SHADOWS
MARC PASTOR

'As gruesome as it is gripping… the writing is extraordinarily vivid… Highly recommended' *Independent*

THE LIBRARIAN
MIKHAIL ELIZAROV

'A romping good tale… Pretty sensational' *Big Issue*

WHILE THE GODS WERE SLEEPING
ERWIN MORTIER

'A monumental, phenomenal book' *De Morgen*

BUTTERFLIES IN NOVEMBER
AUÐUR AVA ÓLAFSDÓTTIR

'A funny, moving and occasionally bizarre exploration of life's upheavals and reversals' *Financial Times*

BY BLOOD
ELLEN ULLMAN

'Delicious and intriguing' *Daily Telegraph*

THE LAST DAYS
LAURENT SEKSIK

'Mesmerising… Seksik's portrait of Zweig's final months is dignified and tender' *Financial Times*

TALKING TO OURSELVES
ANDRÉS NEUMAN

'This is writing of a quality rarely encountered… when you read Neuman's beautiful novel, you realise a very high bar has been set' *Guardian*